There Love Lies

*A Story of Joy, Despair,
and Everything in Between*

By David Ravelo

Inspired Forever Book Publishing
Dallas, Texas

Inspired Forever Book Publishing™
"Bringing Inspiration to Life"
Dallas, Texas
 (888) 403-2727

Printed in the United States of America

ISBN-13: 978-1-948903-00-4

Library of Congress Control Number: 2018952976

Interior artwork created by Mahnaz Ghaleh-Assadi

This book is dedicated to two women who amaze me by their grace, their beauty, and the kindness of their hearts: my mother, Yo-yo, and my daughter, Carla Louella, born seventy-seven years apart, yet, clearly, two peas in a pod.

D. Ravelo
Dallas

"But I awaken always, and forever want to find death
to have my lips remain tangled in your hair."

The Sea Inside, Alejandro Amenábar

Prologue

Abby Miller-Robinson, now living in New York City, came home one late September evening to find the message light on the kitchen phone blinking.

That was odd, as hardly anyone left messages on that number these days other than the occasional sales call.

She absentmindedly hit the play button and glanced through the batch of mail on the counter, simultaneously unraveling from the coat and scarf she had worn that morning to protect her against the cold air that had unexpectedly blown into the city that week.

From the speaker came a voice from long ago. Stunned, she listened.

"Abby. This is Jay Aratta, your dad's friend. It's been years, I know..."

Abby heard hesitancy, a contrast to the voice she remembered. Heavily accented but, until today, always clear, assured, emphatic.

"I got your number from your dad's address book on his computer. I'm sorry to bring bad news, but you have to come to Mexico."

Silence followed as Jay cleared his throat, audibly revealing a man struggling to find words. When he spoke again, the heavy accent she remembered so well was even more apparent.

"Your dad is sick...he's in the hospital, my child. He's had a stroke. Severe. Spoke to the doctor, and it doesn't look good. We might need to take him to Mexico City. I'm staying at his house. I got a call from Rosa, his house caretaker. Call me here. You have the number. Hurry, Abby...he's asking for you."

"Oh, my God," was all Abby could articulate as she lost her breath and her balance, clutching the counter to keep herself from falling.

After living in Texas for more than thirty years, her father had eventually returned to Cuernavaca, a then small city forty miles south of Mexico City. It was not the place where he'd been born, but the town he'd grown up in. But it was filled with memories he perhaps sought to recover, Abby thought to herself as she as she listened to the message once again.

Abby and Thomas, her husband, had accepted job offers in New York around the time her father had decided to move back to Mexico. He had kept his parents' old summer house. Eventually it had fallen into disarray, and in recent years he'd begun fixing it. Abby had visited her grandparents there from time to time when she was just a little girl. Her memory of those times had faded, so her recollections were based on what she saw in the family photo albums. Mostly, they centered on being taught to swim by Keith's father, as a beautiful blonde woman sat close by with a towel. She recognized her grandmother in those photos. At times, a faint memory of her grandmother's scent wafted by.

Abby suspected her dad wanted her to stay in Texas, just a two-hour flight from Mexico City, but New York was a city she loved, and the time had seemed right for her and Tom to move there. They had talked about it for some time, and when things suddenly fell into place professionally, they made the move.

When she saw her dad a few days before he headed south, she had told him about her imminent move to New York City. He seemed to not be surprised by her words as if he'd been expecting them.

"That city has so many great memories for both of us, Abb," he'd told her, a faraway look in his eyes as he recalled the many times he'd taken her there as a child and young woman.

Even as an old woman many years later, Abby would remember the streets, the walks in the snow through Central Park, the dolls and dresses her father had bought her, the late dinners at fancy restaurants after the theater, she wearing a princess costume and her father wearing his bow tie.

"Go make some new memories for yourself, with your husband... and someday with your own children," he'd added.

———————◆◆◆◆◆◆◆◆◆———————

Abby immediately tried calling Jay using an old cell number she had and then her father's home number. When no one answered either number, she went online and booked a flight to Mexico City.

Jay called back late that evening. He tried to sound calm as he explained that her father was receiving the best care possible, but they were words with no meaning that simply filled the empty space between them.

Abby left the following morning after writing Thomas a long to-do list, unaware of how many days she'd be in Mexico. He had offered to join her, but Abby had said no.

"If I need you, I'll let you know, okay?" she had told him. She wanted to show courage, and she also knew this wasn't a good time for him to miss work.

"I'll take the first flight out if you need me. Just call."

"Thank you. I hope it won't be necessary."

As Thomas drove her to the airport, he asked her to give his warm regards to her father.

"I'm sure he'll be fine; it's probably just a little scare," she said, but her concern showed through.

"Honey, it might not be that simple."

"He's old, but he's pretty strong and sharp. I spoke to him just last weekend. He sounded like his old self. He remembers things even I've forgotten."

"I know, my love, but you have to realize that old people get tired and frail in an instant. There doesn't have to be anything seriously wrong. Their bodies simply give up."

"Jesus! Don't get so negative, Thomas. He's going to be fine." Abby's voice sounded harsher than she'd intended.

"I'm not trying to be negative, honey. I just want you prepared. You were there for me when my father died. It meant the world to me, even if I haven't ever said so. I want to be there for you. Part of that is giving each other hope. And part of it is also preparing each other for the inevitable. You have to, Abby."

Abby's face softened. She knew her husband was right. "He always came when I needed him. Now it's my turn. I need to see him, make sure he's okay."

"You will, Abby. You will."

But she didn't.

While Abby dozed on the plane thirty minutes after takeoff at 33,000 feet above sea level, her father peacefully passed away.

When she arrived at the hospital in Cuernavaca later that day, Jay was waiting for her.

He didn't need to say anything for Abby to know that her father was gone. It was in his eyes, in the heaviness of his movements. She saw her father's friend look scared for the first time in his life.

With the tables turned, she now held Jay as he leaned on her shoulder. Inevitably, she began to weep, overcome by her own loss and her father's friend's sadness. Beside her stood the shadow of the man he had once been. Abby remembered her father's good friend as a tall and lean man with an aristocratic air. His black hair slicked back and impeccably dressed in outfits that always seemed out of the ordinary, but that nonetheless looked expensive. And were. She remembered him with a cigarette dangling from his lips, the smile and the twinkle in the eyes of a man who was charming but clearly up to no good. That was Jay. As a child, she had trouble understanding who this man was that brought gifts in beautiful boxes to her and her sisters and brought excitement to her parents who'd prepare for his arrival days in advance.

When Abby went inside that hospital room to see her father, Jay waited outside without being asked.

She sat silently, holding his cold hands. She gazed intently at the closed eyes, the full lips. It was as if looking in the mirror. With the utmost clarity, she could now see where her cheeks had come from. She could see her straight nose in her father's. Her features so much softer, so beautifully feminine, but their resemblance was unmistakable.

The farewell words Abby spoke, she kept to herself. She said what she needed to say, knowing her words would forever eulogize the man she so deeply loved. She kissed his ample forehead and touched his eyelids one last time and walked into the hallway, closing the door behind her.

Almost an hour later, she walked outside the hospital to find Jay sitting on a bench waiting for her. He stood as Abby came to him.

She attempted to dry her eyes, but the tears wouldn't stop.

Jay spoke softly. "He said you were his true north, and then he closed his eyes. You were in his last breath, Abby. Nothing else mattered. You were his happiness."

"He could have waited...why didn't he wait for me? God, why?" Abby collapsed in Jay's arms. These weren't the arms she had come to find warmth in. These weren't her father's arms, nor was this his embrace, but still she felt comforted.

Abby had known Jay since she was born. He had been there an hour after her birth, at her baptism, at countless birthdays, at her graduation from college, and at her wedding. And although he'd been in and out of her and her parent's lives forever, she absently thought that she knew so little about him.

"He tried, Abby. You know he did."

They held each other and let their tears flow without shame, without time, as the shadows darkened and the city softly found its silence.

"He mentioned your mother," Jay continued when he could speak.

Abby didn't say a word, but the shadow of a smile appeared, her expression begging Jay to continue.

"'I might see her up there,' he suddenly said to me."

Jay paused, and Abby was patient, knowing that if anyone could share her pain, it was this old man with the mischievous look whose hair remained jet black to this day.

"I wasn't sure what he meant, Abby. So I asked him."

Another pause. It was as if Jay were trying to be as accurate as possible, as if he knew that every word would be important to Abby, would stay with her for years to come.

"'Who?' I asked him. 'What are you talking about, Keith?' I wasn't sure my friend was thinking clearly. Almost immediately, I saw that he was too emphatic, too clear-eyed, at least at that moment, to be in any way confused."

Jay smiled at Abby. "He said, 'Sam. I might see her up there, Jay. Don't you think? Isn't that what we've always wanted...to know? What happens when we go? Where we go? Wherever it is, I hope she's there,' he whispered. 'You just might see her, Keith,' I told him. 'You just might.'"

"I'm so glad you were there for him, Jay. And I'm glad Rosa called you."

"She said she tried calling you. It was sheer coincidence that I had my phone with me. I often don't." Jay continued, "I came for his birthday five years ago but hadn't seen him since. We spent a great couple of weeks," he recalled. "Jesus, it felt like we were in our twenties again. Not exactly, but we had a great time."

"Do I want to know what you two were up to?"

"Probably not everything, sweetie, but I'll tell you parts sometime."

"You knew him...knew them...when they were young, Jay. You were there when my mom and dad fell in love. What was it like? What were they like?" Abby eagerly awaited his words. They were words that her mother and father had not spoken before. Their stories recounted time after time over the years were always about her as a child, about her growing up. The stories about them, their story as a couple, that...they had locked away after their separation, pretending deftly that it never existed. Abby knew the stories were somewhere in other people's memories of her parents. She was eager to hear Jay tell those seemingly lost stories once more. Jay, like her father, was an amazing storyteller. Perhaps that was the unifying element of their unlikely friendship.

"They were young. Fun. Funny. Crazy. Your mother was gorgeous, and your dad had a way with words. I had the money, but the women fell for your dad. Always."

"Funny! He always told me it was the other way around." A faint smile again played across Abby's lips. "He used to say you were the one always stealing the girls he liked when you both were young."

"We never quite agreed on some things, women being one of them...who we liked, who liked him, who liked me. I hated him sometimes when he got the girl!" Jay said. "But we stayed friends for more than sixty years, actually closer to seventy. He was a pretty crazy man in his own way. When he met your mom and her two girls, your sisters, he fell in love with all three of them, but your mom..."

A faraway look in his eyes, Jay continued reminiscing. "Your parents would sit for hours and talk and drink and laugh and look into each other's eyes and drink some more. Anyone who saw them could tell how much they loved each other, Abby. Your dad really loved your mom. Maybe she never realized how much. Then again, maybe she did and never quite understood why. And there was a time when she loved your dad. That I know as well."

The time felt right to leave. Abby and Jay stood and slowly walked toward the front of the hospital, arm in arm.

"I remember the day I met your mom," Jay told Abby, still reminiscing.

Looking at the old man walking beside her, Abby saw the dark eyes she had always remembered. They sparkled. She sensed his brittleness, his evanescence, could almost feel Jay softly evaporating and drifting away to the day he was describing.

"Your dad told me about meeting this girl named Samantha. I remembered hearing about a girl with that name in Cuernavaca when we were kids. Keep in mind, Cuernavaca was a pretty small town back then, and Samantha was not a very common name. People knew each other."

Abby looked up at Jay expectantly. She wanted the story. Drinking in his words, she noted that his accent, which she'd known since she was a child, was a bit broken, so unlike the soft and deliberate way her father always spoke.

"Your dad asked me to join them for dinner. When I saw your mom, I knew why your dad was so in love. She was all charm, a beautiful woman. But her great trait was that she always seemed so friendly and approachable. She implicitly trusted people, and vice versa. At least that's what she liked people to think."

He stopped to light a cigarette. Abby was about to tell him not to but remembered that it would do no good. He'd smoked for decades and was unlikely to quit now.

"We knocked out three or four bottles of wine at dinner. At least. It was one of those long, long dinners that your parents and I enjoyed every now and then. We'd close the place down, with chairs on the tables and waiters yawning. All I could see was how they looked at each other, how they held hands. It was as if they were accomplices, holding a forbidden feeling that no one else was privy to. Your mom adored your father, and your dad simply floated."

Tears softly fell down Abby's face, but still she smiled. "I wish I could remember them like that," she said, wiping her tears.

"You can, Abby. You were with them. You saw them be happy together. You *made* them happy. Memories are like faith: believing is seeing. Your dad used to say that."

"I think he heard it in a movie. It was funny how he'd remember these little fragments and find hidden meanings in them."

"Yes, he loved words. But more than anything, he loved you, Abby. He always spoke of you, he always made you his center... there was a time when you moved in with him. I guess you were twelve or so...I had tried to get him to go to Spain with me. I knew he could work there, write, maybe even meet a good woman. But he always said he wanted to stay close to you, travel with you. And your mom would never have allowed you to leave Texas. So he stayed because he loved you. And, because he loved Texas too. Although not as much as he loved you."

Abby smiled. "Many of my friends had divorced parents, and they lived with their mothers and their mothers' boyfriends or husbands. I always got a strange look when I told people I lived with my dad. I'm sure I scared off more than one girlfriend of his."

Jay nodded. "I know you did. But...well, he had to do things his own way. Strange man, your father."

"I know. Boy, do I know what a strange man he was at times!" Abby managed another smile that momentarily softened the sorrow pouring from her.

"Strange in a good way," Jay said.

"Strange in a good way," Abby concurred.

"You were everything to him," Jay repeated. "You were his life, Abby. Don't let that thought go. He'll be watching. You know I'm not a big believer, my child, but I think your old obsessive dad will be watching from up there."

"You think, Jay?"

"It doesn't matter what I think. Only you can decide what to believe."

Sorrow as deep as the gray ocean arrived and overtook them, bringing darkness and fear and solitude that touched their souls.

Jay sensed that Abby needed more words, more answers to questions that remained unspoken. "You were born out of great love, Abby. I've always sensed that you believed something different, but I know few children who have been so awaited. There was nothing you or your sisters could have said or done. Your parents made their decisions."

"You might be right, Jay. I just wish I could have asked all the questions I kept inside."

"Your dad told you everything, perhaps too much. He always spoke to you as if you were older, an adult."

"I've always wondered if they loved each other even after they separated."

"I think you know the answer, Abby. Or the answers. There might be several. I have always wondered, just as you have. Why else would your father travel to London to visit your mother's grave after all those years?"

"Travel to London?" Abby was confused. "He never went, Jay...I mean, he did go to London quite a few times, but years and years ago. He might have thought of it after my mom died. I'm sure he thought of it, but he never made it. He couldn't forget; he couldn't *forgive*."

"He did go, Abby. I know he went. He told me."

"When?" Abby wondered if Jay might have misunderstood her father. Her dad would never have gone to London without telling her. He simply wouldn't have.

"Two or three years ago. He called me from London. He wanted me to meet him there. He thought I was in Spain, but I was in Panama at the time...he went to see her...to say goodbye. At least that's what it sounded like."

"He couldn't have. He wouldn't travel all the way to England alone, would he?" Now there was even more doubt in her voice.

"He told me about it several months after he returned. He mentioned the cemetery outside of London; he described the small office building, the soft hills. "He mentioned your mom's burial ground and the black marble headstones—your grandparents' and your mom's side by side. He said there was a pond, a small lake. He said something like, 'I know why she chose that place. It's beautiful and there's peace in the air.' You know...knew...how your dad spoke. Always the romantic, always the poet. He told me the color of the hills, the sounds of the wind...he was there, Abby. Why else would he tell me?"

Abby had been at that cemetery only once, at her mother's burial all those many years ago, but she remembered the hill and her mother's resting place on the soft slope by a pond. She tried to picture the place, and then she realized that the three headstones were in fact black marble. Abby and her sisters had commented on them to each other, but she was certain she had never given her dad those details.

They had seemed so serious, those heavy marble stones, so solemn, so unlike their mother.

Lost in a mountain of confusion and sorrow, Abby murmured, "So he finally went...I didn't know."

"If that helped him sleep and pass on in peace, I'm glad he made the trip," Jay said.

For a moment, emerging from the dark shadow of her dad's death, Abby smiled openly. It was nice to think about her father walking around the hills of that faraway cemetery in the outskirts of London.

Days after the small memorial service for her father had been held in Cuernavaca, Mexico, Abby reflected on how her father's death had coincided with those few weeks in September when a semblance of fall actually touches the leaves, the flowers, the land, and people's hearts, all seeking a respite from the lingering heavy late summer heat.

Her father's few remaining friends had attended. She'd seen Jay sitting silently with Matilda, his daughter, who had come to provide solace to her aging father. She and Matilda had never met before but had liked each other instantly, strangely connected by their fathers' lengthy friendship.

Seeing them side-by-side, Abby had recognized the obvious likeness between father and daughter in their thin noses and the dark puddles of black in their eyes. If anyone could remotely relate to her sorrow, it was Jay, sitting there with his own distant memories.

Abby's Aunt Rose had flown in also. Abby knew her father and her mother's sister had remained friends after her parents had separated. It had been years since Aunt Rose had seen her three nieces together, and she kept beaming at them, a contrast to the somber mood inside the dark, shaded chapel.

Abby recognized other faces but failed to put names to them; they were friends of her father's, she guessed. Some were probably friends from his years in Mexico. She recognized two women her father had dated occasionally years back.

At Keith's passing, word had quickly spread. Abby and Jay had called some people, and some in turn had called others who knew her father. Keith had never been a collector of friends and had few close ones. Of those, some had already passed away. Still, more people had attended than Abby had expected.

Rachel Goetz was one of them. She had approached Abby and her sisters and hugged them warmly and with sincerity. In spite of her age, she was still clearly a beautiful woman. She was impeccably dressed, and Abby couldn't help but notice the stunning jewelry she wore. She had heard about Rachel through both her parents and had met her once or twice over the years. Rachel had gone to school with Abby's mom and dad.

Abby wondered, as she had over the years, if this woman and her father had ever been more than friends. Maybe one day she'd get the courage to ask. Her father had always spoken highly of Rachel.

After looking around the small chapel, Rachel had gone directly to Jay. Seeing the two old friends warmly embrace, Abby had wondered what words they'd exchanged.

Andrea and Emma, Abby's sisters, had arrived two days before the service and had sat by Abby during the mass, all three silently crying next to their aunt, each lost in their memories of the man who had been so present in their youth.

If Keith could have seen them, he would have been reminded of how, as children, they had sought his embrace when the occasional Texas thunderstorm struck, the three of them hiding in his arms, waiting to hear that everything would be all right.

Abby was thankful for those who came. She missed having Thomas by her side, but she had told him to stay in New York. As much as she loved her husband, this was her territory, and she didn't want the added burden of having to guide Thomas or translate the many conversations taking place in Spanish. He would have inevitably felt left out.

The brief ceremony was what her father would have wanted. Abby, Andrea, and Emma had brought in carts of flowers to bring color to every corner of the tiny chapel. This was a touch Abby knew her dad would have liked. He had always sent the girls flowers. Even when they were little, for every recital, every birthday, flowers had arrived.

A Bach Brandenburg Concerto played softly from a dusty and ancient sound system as the small group left the church and gathered briefly outside. Whispered condolences were shared and passed, and soon the volume grew as random encounters brought people together as happens at weddings and funerals.

It was naturally Jay, not letting age or etiquette stand in his way, who broke the silence and somber mood by inviting everyone to Keith's favorite downtown bar for a drink. After all, it was just a few blocks away.

People stood, waiting to see if this was appropriate, so Abby nodded, smiled all around, and began walking by Jay's side, leading the way. A few people bid their farewells, but a small group ambled slowly down the street.

Abby thought again that this was exactly what her father would have wanted. She led the way as they walked in silence to the smoky, dark, and elegant *cantina* for a farewell toast to the man who had left his subtle imprint on all those gathered.

Later that evening, Abby, Andrea, and Emma sat together at their dad's home. Jay had gone to bed, the last few days weighing heavily on him, and the three women sat with a glass of wine, not the first of the evening. Aunt Rose had decided to stay at a hotel even though her nieces had pleaded with her to stay with them.

Although the three women had grown up together, they had not been as close after their respective marriages as they had been when young. Without a doubt, they'd all been affected by the sudden separation of Keith and Sam and the shattered vestiges of their shared life. It was Abby, the youngest, who sought her sisters out from time to time, organizing a get-together, a family reunion, a gathering of some sort.

The awkward silence that crept among them was appropriate for the somber occasion but unnerving nonetheless. They looked at each other silently, seeking words, memories that needed to be dusted off in order to reveal their touching simplicity.

"I remember playing here as kids." Emma finally broke the silence, as she looked at the photographs in the warm living room where they sat. This had been Keith's parents' house, and they had passed it on to their son, but their imprint was apparent.

"We did have some great times," conceded Andrea.

"What's next for you, Abb, now that...he's gone?" Emma asked, wanting to keep the conversation going. There was the ever-present hesitation of what to call Keith. It was as if she'd almost wanted to say "dad." Maybe that was why even Abby had, in her teenage years, begun to call him by his given name.

"I know you guys are leaving the day after tomorrow, so I thought we should get on with a few things that need to be done," Abby began. "I spoke to Jay, and he's seen to my dad's things over the last week since he arrived. You know, lawyer stuff, paperwork. I guess we'll never know if it was coincidence or if Keith somehow knew and asked Rosa to call Jay to come before he passed."

"I'm just glad he's here. He's still funny and so weird," Emma stated.

Abby took a breath, still deep in her hurt. After a moment, she came back to the facts, to the realities death leaves behind for those who stay and live.

"Keith left the house for all three of us. To keep, to sell. Whatever we want to do. Jay has offered to buy it from us. The price is more than fair, and he can pay us all in the next week or so, though God knows why he'd need a house here."

"Are you sure about the house, Abb? You can keep it..." offered Andrea with some hesitation.

"I don't need this house, Andrea. My life...our lives...are elsewhere. The three of us know it. Keith knew it also. He wanted us to have it and to do what we want with his things. He loved us three. Look, I know he didn't call often, but he never stopped loving us."

"You mean he never stopped loving *you*. You were his only daughter, Abby," Andrea attempted to clarify.

"C'mon, Andrea, you know how much he loved you. And Emma."

"He never quite knew how to show it. That's for sure," Andrea insisted.

"The point is, he wanted *us* to have his things. I never thought that I was the only one entitled to his home, his guitars, his books. It's not much, but still...I also know that my dad would have wanted Rosa to have some money. So from the sale of the house, if we all chip in, we can leave her a nice amount to help her out. She's very old, too. She can always leave that money to her children."

"Have you considered that maybe one of us would want to keep the house, Abb?" Emma spoke cautiously, feeling caught in the middle of a slight and unspoken tension between Abby and Andrea.

"It's up to us to decide," Abby replied, "but I think it's pointless to keep it. How often will any of us come here? Do any of us really want to come to Cuernavaca? I think we should accept Jay's offer, and then we can discuss who takes what. There are some paintings; some are surely worth some money. We can ship them to the States and have them appraised if we agree to this. The guitars, I think, we can donate to schools. I might keep one just to have around the house. If we each take one, we can have the rest shipped to the US along with the paintings. Are you okay with that? Emma? Andrea?"

As the two women nodded, Emma said, "I think he'd like the idea of his guitars going to children, but I would like to keep one as well. The small Taylor if it's still around."

"Of course, Emma. I know the one you're talking about. He bought it for you, didn't he? I'm sure it's around here somewhere. Rosa probably knows where everything is."

"It will be a wonderful little memory to keep of Keith."

"You were just as much his daughter as I was. You too, Andrea. I spoke to him all the time, and I know what you both meant to him. Just look around," she urged. "There are photos of the three of us everywhere. This house is filled with memories not of me but of all three of us," she emphasized.

"We all have a part of him in us. And I think he had a bit of us in him as well," Andrea replied quietly.

"We know he did, whether we like it or not," Emma concluded more emphatically, finally smiling a bit.

After a while, the conversation quieted as the fatigue of travel, of sadness, of making arrangements, took its toll.

Perhaps the three sisters wanted to say more, to ask more, but the time didn't seem right. There would be other times, other settings, where they could talk about themselves and Sam and Keith and share their stories of each. Their own collective stories were forever entwined.

For now, they would save their feelings and words for the privacy of their inner conversations, for the intimacy of their dreams.

It was a year and a half before Abby was able to finally take her father's ashes to that familiar ocean on the beach off the coast of central California where she had first touched the sea with her tiny feet, running to it with innocence and awe, immediately running away from it as the low but strong waves came inland to meet her on the soft sand.

He had never told her that this was his wish, but Abby thought it was the ideal place to spread her father's ashes. She knew her parents had come here frequently while they were dating. Later, it was where her father had brought her on vacation.

This was the beach where her father had taught her to swim and to brave the strong breaking waves that came from other lands and other beaches thousands of miles away.

Although she was too young to remember, she forced on herself a memory that this exact beach was where she had last seen her parents hold each other with love, kissing tenderly as the ocean washed their bare feet.

There was a faded photograph of her mother and father somewhere in her closet from which she had conjured this simple memory. They were both so young. Her mother in a minute bright red bikini, legs as long as memories, her blue eyes and blonde hair sparkling in the sun.

Abby had realized at some point in her life that neither she nor her sisters would ever be as beautiful as their mother. This had never bothered her. It was a simple fact she accepted, like the color of her eyes or the beauty mark on her right thigh. Her father always told her she was far more beautiful than her mother. He had his truths. Abby had hers.

In the photograph, her father had the thin lean body of an athlete. His long hair slicked back by the ocean water, he stood slightly behind her mother, his arm draped around her shoulder, both of them deeply tanned.

She and her father had sat on this beach dozens of times as Abby grew up and eventually became a woman.

For years, a picture had been taped to her father's refrigerator of Abby standing on this beach. The picture had faded over the years, but her father had refused to take it down. She had wanted to take it when Jay bought the house, but he had insisted on leaving some of Keith's things as they were.

In the photograph, Abby was probably six, wearing a light blue swimsuit, practicing her ballet steps on the warm sand. She knew her father loved that simple photograph, but she wasn't sure why.

Now, she would never know, and that was okay. She didn't need all the answers. The ones she had would suffice. The rest were questions that perhaps simply had no answers.

As Abby sprinkled her father's remains, a gust of wind played with her blonde hair and scattered the powder, which eventually fell and became part of the same sand where he had walked with her.

Then she sat on the beach and looked at the horizon. Just as she had when she was four and had sat there with her father almost fourty years ago, she wondered what was on the other side of that immense blue ocean.

Chapter 1

J uly 10 was a special day for Keith. It was his birthday.

Birthdays had never been of any importance to him. They merely represented one more year and how much further he felt from beginnings, how much closer he felt to endings, as life went by.

Sure, he had enjoyed the girls' birthdays growing up. He enjoyed their eyes shining in anticipation, the countdown toward *the day* that sometimes started months before, shopping for their gifts, but his own birthday he had dismissed as simply one more day.

Yet in the last few months or so, he had actually begun to look forward to this particular July 10. It was partly the excitement of turning seventy-four, but even more it was the anticipation of the visit from his old friend Jay and Jay's birthday coming two days later.

He had received the email a month before saying Jay would arrive in Mexico on July 10 and would come straight from the airport to Cuernavaca.

Keith was doubtful the date Jay had chosen to visit had anything to do with their birthdays, but he could never be certain when it came to Jay. What mattered was that he'd see his friend.

The two men hadn't spent time together in quite a few years. The last time they'd met was an accidental encounter in New York City. What a night that had been! Except for the occasional email and the less and less frequent calls, he knew little about what Jay been doing or where he'd been living.

Keith missed his friend. He knew he was missed as well. They'd been friends for so long that, of all the people in the world, it was unquestionably Jay who knew him best.

In addition to having the soul of a vagabond, Jay had an almost magical way of extracting Keith's thoughts at any given moment, dissecting in a flash his attitude, and giving him the crispest possible answers to questions he hadn't even asked. Jay cut through the layers of meanings with precision, grace, and eloquence. No bullshit, no holds barred. It could actually be a bit eerie.

Keith knew they would talk about the future. Jay loved the future: there was always an adventure to embark on, an enigma to decipher, the drawing on a map pointing the path to new hungers.

Jay was also always in motion, whether physically pacing aided by his lifelong love of cocaine or mentally going back and forth in a private world of strange and buzzing ideas.

The pair had met when they were eleven and twelve, Keith older by a year and two days. Keith had walked by the big house with the tennis court quite a few times. It was only two blocks away from his home.

On a few occasions, he had seen the kid with jet-black hair walking aimlessly around the enormous garden or playing tennis against a wall by himself. Keith would have loved to play, but he never worked up the courage to talk to the kid behind the fence.

One day the boy said hi and asked Keith if he wanted to come in and play.

He'd walked in, gazing in awe as the boy led him through the enormous house, finally reaching the expansive and exquisitely kept garden. These were not details captured by the young Keith, who only made a mental note comparing the size of his house to this mansion.

In the small gazebo by the court, Keith found a basket with all types of rackets, all expensive and virtually brand new.

"What's your name?" the boy asked as he bounced the ball that lazy afternoon.

"Keith. I live a bit down the avenue. What's yours?"

"What's my what?"

"Your name."

"I'm Jay."

Keith always remembered that first encounter. He had a clear mental picture of Jay as a kid: long, straight, razor sharp nose, unruly black hair, and eyes that were always dancing from one thing to another. And that attitude, part enchantment, part arrogance, with which he charmed people.

Although the last time Keith had seen Jay he had gray hair at the temples and deep lines etched into his skin, the thin, lean face had remained the same along with the sense of urgency with which he had lived all his life. Impatient always.

After playing for a bit, they'd sat by the court in silence.

"Well, I gotta go," said Keith. "Here's your racket."

"Keep it. Just bring it back tomorrow and we'll play again."

"What if I don't come back and keep your racket?"

"I'll come and get it."

"You don't even know where I live."

"Yes, I do. I've seen you around. You play really good."

"I play with my dad a lot. Who do you play with?"

"You, now."

"I meant normally."

"Whoever. The chauffeur, my cousins when they visit, other kids who come to visit with their parents."

"So why all the rackets?"

"They're just there for people to use. My dad bought them for me."

"Wow, that's a lot of rackets."

"There's a few that haven't ever been used. You can keep the one you used today."

"No, no. I'll bring my own. I'm used to it. Okay. I'll see you around."

"Tomorrow?"

"Aren't you going to ask your parents if it's okay?"

"They aren't here," Jay replied.

"Are they working?"

"No. They're traveling."

"Oh, so when do they get back?"

"I'm not sure. A week or so."

"Do you have brothers or sisters?"

"Why?"

"No reason. Just curious. This is a really big house, that's all. Huge."

"No brothers or sisters. Just me and my parents." After a pause, he added, "When they're here."

"Well, okay," Keith said, not knowing what else to say.

"So, tomorrow?"

"Sure," Keith said as he walked into the street and headed home.

Walking back to his house, Keith thought it was funny that he'd met a friend who played tennis and who also happened to have a name that could never be properly pronounced in Spanish.

Jay would invariably be called *Yey*, as the English *J* sound did not quite exist, while Keith would forever be *Kid* in Spanish, which sounded almost like *Keed*, since the English *th* sound didn't exist in Spanish. He also sometimes was called *Kate*, following the literal pronunciation of his name in Spanish, the *ei* sounding like an English open *a*, as in *cake*.

There were times when Jay and Keith, each in his own mind, wondered what their parents were thinking when they'd named them, or at least what they were thinking when they'd moved them to Mexico.

They didn't know it then, but a friendship of a lifetime formed that afternoon. Although they didn't go to the same school, they lived close to each other, which made it easy to spend time together. Unlike other friendships made up of shared experiences, shared places, or shared friends, Jay and Keith's friendship was more of a crisscrossing of paths through different periods in life, unexpected encounters that propelled the two to remain inextricably connected.

It was years before Keith realized that Jay's parents were distant, abstract figures who came and went, traveling incessantly. Over the course of years, he met them many times.

The father was a Spanish expatriate, tall and intense like his son with an unmistakable *madrileño* accent, the mother a vague, blonde, and beautiful woman. She was American and spoke Spanish with the accent she'd picked up after years in Spain. There was an air of easy living, of assured affluence, to Jay's family, yet they always felt disassociated from each other, distant.

This was very different from Keith's relationship with his own parents, with whom he remained close until their passing. With his brother Tony, Keith had a somewhat less close relationship. Their paths crossed only occasionally, but they always found a warmth and connection that might not sizzle but was always there, with its ebb and flow and undercurrents.

Keith had long ago perceived a sense of solitude in Jay that he'd learned not to question. It was that need for solitude that made Jay the lifelong vagabond he became. In spite of his incredible intellect, there was always a fear, an insecurity, just below the surface that kept him moving, not wanting to be tied to friends, a single woman, a single place.

As he drifted back to the present, Keith reminded himself that, with Jay, there was never ever any looking back. It was always tomorrow and beyond tomorrow, just as it had been during their first conversation almost sixty-three years before.

Keith wanted to look back during this visit. He wanted to remember. He wanted to see his friend's view of the many years they'd shared. The celebrations, too many to count; the friends, men and women, also too many to count; the moves from city to city, from country to country; the disappointments and even the deaths of friends whose farewells still lingered and hurt.

As he pored over his memories, Keith realized they were woven into the *enredadera* and the moss that covered the walls of his home and the other walls of this city. The walls that hid the homes, the rooms, the terraces where their lives had taken place. It seemed that these walls played games. You walked behind one as a child and came out the other side older, slower in movement, hopefully a bit wiser.

Behind these walls, Keith knew, was the story of a boy and a girl. It was a simple and very ordinary story of chance encounters, hearts entwined and then set free, years gone by, and memories that cast shadows that were dry and warm as the brick beneath Keith's feet.

It was a story that had a well-defined beginning yet no apparent ending. Keith had wished many a time that it would end, but he himself perpetuated it, reinvented it, and rediscovered himself in it.

Like all the stories we cherish, the ones that revive some long hidden sadness or bring us unending joy, sometimes a bit of both, this story of a boy, Keith Miller, and a girl, Samantha Riley, had stayed with him through the years.

This day, his birthday nonetheless, waiting to see his friend of a lifetime, Keith let his eyes look far into the green foliage that surrounded the house. Soon his heart and breath followed his gaze to the years gone by, those both far and near.

Coming out of his reverie, he checked the clock. It was 9:32 a.m. He ate breakfast, read the newspapers, and took a morning swim, then slept lightly for an hour on one of the soft couches on the terrace.

He finally went in, took a shower, and dressed. When the cab he had called came to pick him up, it was almost 1:30, the sun shining bright and heavy on the city of eternal spring.

Chapter 2

Although they were born thousands of miles apart, Keith Miller and Samantha Riley grew up in the same small town. The strange alignment of the stars brought their families to Cuernavaca for different reasons and several years apart.

Samantha arrived when she was seven and her sister Rose was almost twelve. Their father, Charles Riley, had been a businessman in London all his life. After several failed endeavors, he had started a small pub in the outskirts of London that had become a hit.

That small restaurant and bar had gradually become two, and then a small chain had spread across London and its surroundings. Charles Riley was a tall, thin, and handsome man of simple needs and few words who was perpetually baffled by the financial success his pubs had suddenly bestowed on him and his family.

Samantha's mother, on the other hand, had always felt entitled to a better life than her husband had provided, at least until now. Tall like her husband, she was a full-figured woman with an abrupt manner and piercing blue eyes that revealed her intelligence and were capable of instilling respect in others.

As their wealth increased with each passing year, she took charge of the books. She proved to have great business acuity and invested their money wisely. She also decided where they should live, where they should shop, and where their daughters should attend school.

This arrangement worked well for the couple and gave Charles the time he desired to visit the family's outposts, talk kindly to customers, and sit in a corner booth for hours on end with a good book and an equally good glass of whiskey. His wife bustled about the office and their home with a perpetual need to accomplish, earn, or arrange.

It was through a friend of hers that Nelly Riley heard of the small town of Cuernavaca in Mexico. Her friend, also British, had planned to visit the area with her husband for a few weeks but had ended up staying, charmed by the friendliness of the people and the beauty of the homes hidden behind stone walls.

With her great determination driving her, Nelly crossed the Atlantic to Mexico for the first time in her life to see for herself the charms of the small city she had heard so much about.

She flew her family to Mexico City during the December holiday and then traveled with them by car to Cuernavaca. The thick green foliage, the abundance of flowers, and the beautiful weather impressed her, but it was the constantly smiling people who struck her as incredible.

It was evident that many of the people in the streets were poor, yet there was an undeniable peace and joy in their dark eyes. There was also a willingness to stop whatever they were doing to begin a celebration. This was such a sharp contrast to the dreary weather and unshakeable prudence and correctness of her compatriots in her native England that Nelly immediately decided to follow in her friend's footsteps and move to Mexico.

Six months later, she convinced her husband that Cuernavaca was the place to raise the girls and where they could spend a life of leisure funded by their businesses in England. Charles Riley knew there was nothing he could do to change his wife's mind, so he handpicked his best managers and left them in charge of the twelve pubs and restaurants he now owned.

In the seventh month of the year, the Riley's sold their house and returned to Cuernavaca to find a suitable home. Nelly marched in and out of eleven homes before she decided on *their* home. It was a house that showed some traits of the traditional Mexican colonial style with vaulted brick ceilings, hand-painted tile, and such, but the house blended these elements with the aesthetics of more contemporary European architecture, boasting huge open spaces and clean interior lines.

Although they seldom agreed, Charles and Nelly Riley both adored their home from the very first day. They also loved their girls, both blonde, tall, and with fine features that combined the chiseled looks of their father with the softness of their mother's mouth and the bright blue eyes both parents shared.

The young girls quickly found themselves immersed in school. They didn't speak Spanish, but they soon learned this new language and new way of life complete with Spanish-speaking friends, a pool, servants, and dogs.

After their first six months, they seldom spoke of their friends and former life across the ocean.

Keith's father and mother both were teachers. Troy Miller and Marisa Silverstein had met at UCLA during the last few months of completing their master's degrees. They'd gone out a few times but were undecided as to their next steps, so their benign fondness for each other didn't lead to anything.

Troy accepted a teaching post at a private boy's school in Texas upon graduation while Marisa returned home to her parents in San Francisco. They stayed in touch, and in their letters back and forth, they discovered their shared interest in Mexico.

Troy's father had spent some years in Mexico working for a textile company and had moved his family there for three years. That experience had inspired a love of the language in young Troy and given him wonderful memories of the many deserted beaches and mountains they visited.

Marisa's mother had spent a couple of summers as a young woman in Guadalajara visiting distant relatives. Years later, while living in San Francisco, she occasionally took Marisa to Guadalajara on long road trips, cruising the vast valleys, deserts, and sierras that separated these two distinct and distant cities.

In Mexico City, where each moved to explore teaching positions at various universities, Marisa and Troy began spending time together. Their love of teaching, of children, and of Mexican life brought them steadily together. It was as if the land itself was inextricably weaving them together.

They returned to the US for a few years where they eventually married and gradually started a family, bought a home, and settled into the comfortable life of Southern California, but they both knew that eventually Mexico, with its wonderful people and places, would come calling. Years later, when it did, they jumped. They missed the chaos, the propensity for celebrations absent in their tranquil California lifestyle.

With two boys in tow, Anthony age thirteen and Keith eleven, they returned to Mexico City. Troy began teaching at a large private university in the southern section of the city while Marisa juggled two growing boys and a part-time job teaching English to Mexican employees at the US Embassy.

A few years later, the Morelos State University in Cuernavaca knocked on Marisa's door seeking someone to head its literature department. She accepted the offer on the spot, knowing her husband would be delighted to see her pursue her own career and knowing he'd be interviewed at the same school in the coming weeks.

To Marisa's delight, Troy also got the job. To the day they retired, they drove together to and from work and sat together almost every day under the shade of the campus trees, sharing lunch and passing each other sections of the city's daily newspaper, *Diario de Morelos*.

After being hired, and immediately after the boys' school let out for the summer, Marisa began visiting Cuernavaca on the weekends, seeking a place to live. Keith often accompanied her while Anthony and Troy stayed in the city.

After several consecutive weekends with no success and the clock ticking towards the end of summer, Marisa and Keith drove once again outside the Mexico City valley and into the warmth of the city of eternal spring.

The second house they saw that morning became theirs. When Keith and his mom walked into the Mexican colonial house, each of them knew, without saying a word, that this was where they would live. Although the house had recently been built, it felt as though shadows and ghosts and stories already inhabited it. Without question, it was their role to add the Miller family stories and leave their imprint on this home.

Keith's mother didn't have to say anything. Keith sensed, rather than observed, the quiet, almost seductive, way his mom glanced at the open living and dining areas, the way she peered into the kitchen. Keith knew his mom well enough to know that she had already made a mental note of where the furniture would go, of what would fit where.

They slowly walked up the stairs. Listening to the echo of their footsteps, Keith imagined the richness and clarity of playing his guitar here. He had turned eleven a few days earlier, and there was nothing he loved more than his guitar.

As if they had rehearsed it, mother and son walked into the two adjoining rooms. His mom walked through the door on the right while Keith chose the left.

If someone had seen them walk the rooms simultaneously, they would have noticed an uncanny similarity in how they opened closets, peeked inside the showers of their respective bathrooms, felt the newness and coolness of the hand-painted tiles.

They also burst onto the balconies with the wrought iron railings at the same time. They smiled to each other in surprise as they stepped into the bright sun illuminating each balcony.

"It's beautiful," Keith heard his mother say.

They stood for a moment, gazing at the beautiful garden in front of them. At that moment, they unknowingly made the first shared family memory to live in this house.

Keith's father would pass away many years later on the terrace below. He would slip away as he always said he would, lying in his hammock in his shorts, sipping rum and reading a mystery novel that he'd likely read at least three times before, slowly and inevitably remembering who had committed the murder.

On this day, they left the house after Keith's mother had asked all the pertinent questions of the real estate lady.

Apparently, the price was right. Keith had seen his mom walk out of a few extremely large homes, liking them but discounting them on the spot. He was too young to fully understand, but he sensed these homes were beyond his parents' means.

His mom was pensive as they took the road back to Mexico City. After more than an hour of near silence, as they pulled into the driveway, she asked, "Did you like that house we saw?"

Without hesitation, Keith replied, "I think it's very nice."

"I think it's the one," his mother stated as she turned off the ignition and stepped out of the car.

A few months later, right before the start of Keith's sixth grade school year, just two years after the Riley family arrived from England, Troy, Marisa, Tony, and Keith Miller arrived, too.

The small town back then was a paradise, yet Keith hated it at first. Coming from a big private Catholic school in the big city, he felt intensely out of place in the tiny new school with its small dirt patio to spend recess in. The school had no sports activities and no soccer team, something unheard of where he'd come from.

To further cement his initial hatred of this new geography, of his parents, of his brother, and of life in general, there was no television signal at their new house. When a kid is eleven, he can lose his best friends, he can lose his beloved soccer team, he can lose the girl across the street with whom he's secretly in love, but an eleven-year-old boy cannot lose his television.

Nonetheless, time allowed him to adjust. Lo and behold, little by little, Keith learned to love his new town, and he got to know it well. To this day, he knows many a street that few people have ventured into, and he got to know Cuernavaca the way one always gets to know cities: by walking them.

He walked and walked and walked the streets.

With their parents immersed in teaching and no bus service to school, Tony and Keith had to fend for themselves. Tony quickly made friends and most days got a ride with a neighbor. Keith would ride to school with them, but elementary and middle school let out at different times, so he usually came out after school only to find that Anthony had already left for home.

Eventually, Keith discovered the city buses. He loved trying different routes, walking block after winding block and getting on buses, not knowing where that particular route would end.

He'd ride it to the end of the line, normally in some isolated dirt parking area filled with tires, strewn tools, and stray dogs lying in the shade under the buses, seeking solace from the blistering sun. There, in the shade of a small shabby cover, bus drivers would congregate, commenting on the last inter-city crossing, drinking the big bottled beers, *caguama*, and smoking *Delicados sin filtro*.

Keith would wait for a departing bus to eventually leave the improvised depot. The wait could be as short as five minutes or as long as an hour and a half. Schedules were unheard of, and since by this time it was close to three in the afternoon., he often had a long wait since the city simply ceased all movement from 2:00 to 4:00. It was time to eat, unbuckle belts, and sleep until the shade of the afternoon and the rain cooled the inhabitants enough for them to cautiously take to the streets once again.

As the heat passed and the rain became a light, fresh sprinkle, the city would gradually awaken from its slumber. The storefronts would open, the balloon vendors would begin circling the plaza, the cars would honk loudly once again, and the food stands selling corn and *ezquites* would reawaken as passersby stopped, inevitably tempted by the vapors of the boiling corn escaping the metal kettles.

Keith thrust himself into the city, intent on knowing every street, exploring every smell. On occasion, he visited the central market.

It was a maze of pottery, flowers, food, and carcasses that merged into a mass of heat and smells he would never forget.

Every corner, every passage, was an adventure. Years later, the central market became surrounded by newer stands and street vendors peddling pirated movies and CDs, TVs, the latest in pirated footwear, perfumes, and toys plus whatever gadget was hot that month.

By sheer coincidence, Sam and Keith ended up at the same school. Letting his mind wander, Keith was immediately back in the sixth grade, looking up from the schoolyard toward the classrooms, when he saw the girl leaning against the rail.

For a moment, he thought she was looking at him. Maybe she was. She was wearing a light blue dress and the sun shone brightly on her blonde hair. She smiled at him without hesitation, and he smiled back.

From that moment on, Keith never forgot her. At that particular moment, he turned to his new friends and classmates, Charlie and Alberto.

Without him formulating the question, just by following Keith's gaze to the girl by the rail, they answered his unasked question almost in unison. "That's Samantha Riley."

Charlie, who was much more knowledgeable in the ways of the world and more *macho*, repeated, "Samantha Riley. That's a stupid name. Why would your parents name you Samantha? Most of her friends call her Sam. Shit, that's a boy's name. But she is a fox. I'll bet she sucks cock. All these *gringas* do."

Keith wasn't sure what Charlie was talking about but nonetheless said without conviction, "Yeah."

Alberto, much more emphatically, declared, "No, she doesn't. She's only ten, you know? Plus, she's not a *gringa*, she's from England, you fat asshole."

"Whatever, squirt! And if she doesn't suck dick, then I'll teach her!"

Alberto pushed Charlie and Charlie shoved him back, giving him a look that implied an answer like that could get him in some deep shit.

"Dream on," was all Alberto could say to avoid a confrontation.

"Yeah, well, then you'll suck my cock, won't you, faggot?" Charlie said, swatting Alberto hard on the back of the head.

"Have your sister do it, asshole. She's really good at it," Alberto taunted, not backing down in spite of the difference in size between them.

"You little shit!" Charlie yelled.

"C'mon, you guys!" Keith moved forward, between them. "Stop messing with each other! Sometimes you're like little five-year-olds."

Alberto started laughing. Charlie, caught off guard, joined in, and the moment of tension passed.

Charlie, clearly accustomed to bossing people around, was a tall, beefy boy with freckles and a huge moon face.

Alberto was a shaggy-haired blond kid almost a head shorter than Charlie.

Keith was the missing link. Right in the middle of the other two in terms of height, he wasn't as belligerent as Charlie but was a bit more of a bad boy than Alberto. The three became good friends that year although they went to different schools afterward and rarely crossed paths again.

A few days later, during the first weeks of school, Keith learned of the existence of another girl, Rachel Goetz. She was pretty, with black hair and light eyes. She was always smiling but a bit of a loner, Keith later realized.

Rachel was also a bit tomboyish. She spent most of her time with the boys, playing soccer and hanging out with them without the self-consciousness most other girls displayed.

Keith remembered a conversation he had with her, Charlie, and Alberto one day. As usual, Charlie's way of showing affection was by rudely asking questions.

"So, Rachel, how come you just hang around us instead of going over there and sitting with the rest of the girls? Don't they like you?"

"Nah, they just talk about boys. I'd rather *be* with boys. Most of those girls are so stupid."

"Well, we really don't want you here. We're going to talk about guy things," Charlie said in his typical rude fashion.

"And what would that be? Jerking off? I know all about that from my older brother and his friends."

"You are so weird. C'mon, we don't want you here. Do we guys?" Charlie looked around for support. Neither Keith nor Alberto knew what to say. They liked Rachel.

"Yes, you do. You're just too dumb to know it," she threw right back at him.

"Let her be, Charlie," Keith intervened.

"Yeah," Alberto echoed.

"You three are so stupid and immature, especially you, Charlie," Rachel stated as she stood up, brushed off her jeans, and walked away. Ten years old, smiling in victory, her face shone with confidence.

"Do you always have to be so stupid?" Alberto asked Charlie.

"Shut up, faggot!"

As the three boys watched her walk away, each attempted to make sense of the words spoken by that odd girl. It was perhaps the first time in their lives that they realized there would always be something in women that was just around a corner they would never take, a slight enigma they would never fully understand.

Although Keith enjoyed Rachel's company, it was Samantha who moved him off center. It was as if she exercised a pull on his thin frame that made him sway to the side as she passed by and then drew him into her wake. All this he felt without speaking to her once.

Since Sam was in the fifth grade and Keith in the sixth, their contact was limited to the awkward and uncomfortable moments when they bumped into each other in a hallway. Eventually, Sam said hi. A few days later, Keith found the courage to start a brief conversation.

"I heard Charlie say you're from England. Really?"

"Charlie? The big kid in your class?"

As soon as she spoke, Keith could hear the accent. "That's him. Hard to miss him."

"I should say. His sister is my friend, you know."

"I guess you are from England, even if you didn't say so. You sound...English."

"London. Well, right outside of London, really."

"Wow! I wish I could go there," Keith blurted.

"Really? Why?"

He fumbled for an answer. "I don't know...I guess...Good music?" He instantly thought of his brother Tony's records of bands like the Stones, the Beatles, The Who.

Sam laughed. This was such a wonderful sound that Keith wanted to hear it again, but instead of saying anything, he just stood there gradually turning red.

"Good music? That's a good one, really. So, you like music?" She smiled at Keith, who wanted this moment to last as long as possible.

"Yeah," he answered nervously, not wanting to be caught with another question he couldn't answer.

"You play an instrument?"

"A little guitar. I'm taking lessons."

"You speak such good English. How come? American?"

"Well, yes, but..." He was a bit surprised by her curiosity and her willingness to talk to him.

"Yes...?"

"I was born—" he began just as the bell rang, so he said nothing else.

As she walked away, he said, "By the way, I'm Keith."

"Sure, Keith Miller. You're the new kid. I know that," she answered, turning toward him for a moment before just as quickly turning away and walking down the hall.

These little encounters became a bit more frequent, and Keith and Sam began to look for each other coming out of class, by the small cafeteria, in the hallways, and on the small, dusty playground.

Sometimes, as recess began, they would stand together looking down at the playground. They were about the same height, Sam just a bit taller, and they leaned against the rail while their respective friends chatted about the boys beginning to pick teams for the inevitable game of soccer on the dusty makeshift field and the girls sitting around giggling at God knows what, always pretending to ignore the boys chasing the ball.

Although neither Sam nor Keith could remember what they said to each other, the words were likely few and a bit unintelligible, even a bit brutal. At that age, there is little room for charm and more fertile territory to tease and shock.

Invariably, someone would notice their absence from their usual groups and they would be interrupted by the teasing and laughter of her friends or the mocking yells from his, incapable of understanding why he'd rather hang around Samantha Riley than get down in the dirt, ready to kick the ball in the thick summer heat.

One day, after walking away from Samantha and joining Charlie and Alberto, Keith realized he'd happened into a conversation about an upcoming party being held by one of their classmates.

"So, did you ask her?" asked Charlie with a big grin.

"Ask who what?" Keith replied.

"Sam."

Keith looked uncertainly at Charlie and Alberto.

"If she's going to Leticia's party on Saturday, what else, Miller?" Alberto asked.

"No. Are you guys going?" Keith wasn't even aware of the party but didn't want to reveal that fact.

"I am," chimed in Alberto. Little son of a bitch was quiet, but he always knew what was up.

"Who the fuck invited you?" Charlie asked with his exaggerated bad attitude.

"Leticia did; who else?"

"Are you going?" asked Keith, still the newest member of their little boy's club.

"I'm not sure," replied Charlie, older, wiser, cooler than either Alberto or Keith, implying with his tone that perhaps his schedule wouldn't permit it. "Why don't you come to my house, and we can walk over to Leticia's from there. It's only two blocks from my house," Charlie offered once he'd reconsidered.

"Sure," said Alberto.

"I was talking to Keith," Charlie hissed.

"Stop being an asshole, Charlie."

Keith wasn't sure when they were teasing each other or why they were even friends, yet they seemed inseparable.

"So, will you come over?" Charlie asked again, looking at Keith.

"Sure. When?"

"We'll all meet at 4:00 at Charlie's on Saturday," Alberto concluded, clearly unruffled.

"Great," said Keith, and he meant it.

The soccer ball rolled to them and off they went. Three boys who for a fraction of a second had tasted potential maturity were again just three sweaty boys chasing a soccer ball in a cloud of dust.

A day later, as school let out, Keith exited the boy's bathroom and almost collided with Samantha in the hallway.

Without any apparent reason, his face turned red on the spot. Again.

"Hey, are you going to Leticia's on Saturday?" she asked with that particular way of making her words sound half invitation and half taunt.

"Are you?" he came back cautiously.

"I asked first."

"Maybe. You?"

"Maybe."

"Okay, I'll go if you're going. But if you have other plans..."

"Keith, I'm going. It's no big deal. And next time we meet, you probably shouldn't turn red. Someone might get the idea that you like me. We can't have that, can we?"

His face turning even redder than before, he turned to watch her walk away. For the briefest moment, she looked back at him and smiled. He smiled back, certain he could smell the slight aroma of gum and soap in her wake.

In those brief moments, Keith discovered what a girl's hair blowing in the breeze, combined with a subtle smile, can do to a boy. In those fragments of time with Samantha Riley, he took imaginary snapshots of her smile, of her blue eyes, of her long, tanned legs as she stood by that rail in that blue summer dress she was so fond of wearing.

Although he didn't know it at the time, those faint flashes of joy would remain with him forever.

The party at Leticia's was unfamiliar territory. Keith played most of the afternoon with Charlie and Alberto. Around 4:30, they walked to the party. They were some of the first guests to arrive, and they exchanged greetings with Leticia's parents, who were hovering about.

The girls in their classroom arrived about half an hour later. Sam arrived late wearing an orange dress and black shoes. Keith had seen her walk in but pretended he hadn't, not wanting to appear too eager. He tried his best, but it was hard not to notice her bare legs.

She immediately came to Keith and said without preamble, "Hi, Keith. Are you going to dance with me later?"

"I...I think...I don't...Yes!" he recovered with some dignity.

"Good. That's why I came. But it can't be the slow songs. My dad won't let me dance to those. Okay?"

"Okay," he answered, unsure of what that meant but sensing there was some hidden message and clearly willing to abide by whatever rules of engagement she set.

"Bye, Keith. See you inside. Remember, I'm the one with the orange dress."

"Don't worry, Samantha. I'll find you," he fumbled.

"Don't take too long. By the way, almost everyone calls me Sam. You should try it," she smiled coyly.

"We'll dance in a while, Samantha. Sam, I mean."

"I'd hate to end up dancing with your friend Charlie and have you miss your chance. Anyway, I think Spin the Bottle is about to start," she tossed over her shoulder as she ran into the house and the music inside. She moved like a young colt, a bit awkwardly, as if getting used to her long, growing legs.

After a second, Keith ran in behind her.

As the summer turned to fall and then to winter, just as boys and girls have done since the beginning of time, they danced a few songs, spoke a few words, and, furtively one day, held hands.

Above all, they began to like each other more and more, this boy Keith Miller and this girl Samantha Riley. Nonetheless, it would take them more than twenty years before they realized that children's dreams sometimes do come true.

Chapter 3

Keith arrived in downtown Cuernavaca on this particular July 10, paid the cab driver, and began to walk the streets of his old hometown. Anxious with the anticipation of Jay's arrival, Keith had decided to visit the old historic area of downtown Cuernavaca. It had gotten him out of the house and out of Rosita's, his house caretaker's, way as she prepared dinner and made up the guest bedroom.

But, above all, it was in these small streets that he had come over the years to perhaps get a sense of where he truly belonged. Although he'd always felt very American, this city had left a mark on his life as it had on Jay's and Sam's. Funny how none of them had been born here, yet here their lives had accidentally intertwined.

He heard the cathedral bells ring the hour in the distance. It was 2:00 p.m. on the dot. As he walked along the narrow sidewalks, he inevitably moved into the past.

Each street he passed was filled with memories of his youth, of his friends, and of Sam. Most of the stores had changed but the buildings remained, older, shabbier, but still proudly looking onto the square where children still ran in delight and where the very poor still begged for money with the look of resignation of hundreds of years of want.

Just as Nelly Riley, Sam's mother, had found a hidden friendliness in the people she saw, so did Keith. He could look past the poverty and see the amazing and simple joy so easily expressed in the dark, dancing eyes of the people of this city. Just as the sadness and wanting was millennial, so was their happiness, passed from generation to generation and discovered in the simplest of moments.

But while the soul of its people had not changed, Cuernavaca, he sadly realized, had. The beauty it once reflected had vanished as the streets became impossibly littered and the pollution from the neighboring factories and countless buses brought a permanent grayish halo through which the ever-present spring weather still could be felt.

The city still sloped down the mountains in the north and expanded into what had once been beautiful green hills, but these were now covered by the gray labyrinth of half-paved streets connecting development after development, absent of any planning, just springing out of nowhere as land was invaded by people settling in the city's periphery, desperately seeking a place to call home and make their meager living.

On the northeastern side of the city, the beautiful mountains leading to Tepoztlán were visible behind the smoky skies while, to the west, the city's inhabitants gradually usurped the fertile hills that led to Chalma and towns beyond that.

To the south, the city had grown far past the city limits, now overflowing into the valleys where roses and sugar cane had grown for centuries. Continuing south down the highway, the valleys again became mountains, later descending and softly ending on the coastal palm-filled hills that overlooked the sea.

It was one hundred and eighty kilometers from Cuernavaca to the warmth and brine of the majestic Pacific Ocean, but it was downtown Cuernavaca that Keith considered his epicenter. The area was loosely defined as the blocks between Humbold and Obregón Avenues, as the east and west boundaries respectively.

The streets on the north began at the church of El Calvario and ran south for about fifteen blocks to Abasolo. The streets were tiny and insufficient for the growth of the city and the countless vehicles transiting in chaos, yet, to this day, Keith felt drawn to them, as he had when he was a kid, perhaps enjoying his newly found independence more than the streets themselves.

The innermost downtown area remained unchanged, formed by the two main squares. The smaller Zócalo still retained its old kiosk as well as the balloon vendors and *boleros* who sat on their stools, shining countless shoes and boots to perfection. It all remained as if time had never passed.

On Sundays, the municipal band played on instruments even older than the men who played them, if that was possible. The larger Plaza de Armas was an open *esplanade* perpetually filled with protesters of some sort, running children, and street vendors.

It had changed over the years, with each successive governor adding a small distinctive and ugly detail: a new clock that never worked quite as accurately as it was supposed to; new stands for artisans to sell their wares that regrettably seemed more and more assembly-line made; new trees planted with the good intention of providing more shaded areas but inadvertently increasing the chances of bird shit landing on someone's head.

"Where has all its beauty gone?" Keith asked himself.

Almost at the right angle corner of both plazas stood the Palacio de Gobierno, the state government seat, a large gray and brown building into which people entered, invariably carrying manila folders under their arms containing documents of immense importance to someone. In all the years Keith had lived in and visited this city, he had never once been inside. In fact, he didn't know anyone who had.

Across the plaza, the Cortez Palace stood gallantly defying the passing of the centuries, having been built as the summer retreat of the once mighty *conquistador* over five centuries before. It still remained proudly well kept and housed beautiful murals and fragments of the town's long history as the small, sunny sister to the sprawling Mexico City and its Mexica predecessor, Tenochtitlán, to the north.

In spite of its new facades and its pollution, Cuernavaca was still the city of Keith's past, and so it became the perfect setting to continue exploring that distant past before it faded like the color from the brittle brick roofs.

Before Jay arrived, Keith was determined to re-examine, to relive on this birthday, the days he'd spent with Sam and the girls growing up. He had kept the memories locked inside for years. Perhaps it was time for those stories to be let out, to find their path into the very streets where they had taken place.

Even though he desired Jay's point of view, Keith knew these memories could only be experienced by himself alone. He felt as if he were seeking answers that might lie in the dusty corners or on the sidewalks of these streets.

Off he went, striding slowly with seventy-four years on his back, into yet another winding street that opened yet another memory that suddenly became sharper and closer than ever before.

He reached the entrance to a familiar restaurant. It was as if his feet had brought him here on their own, retracing the steps he'd taken four decades earlier to his first date with Samantha.

He didn't go in. Instead, he peered into the open patio through the windows facing the street. People were busy setting up tables and aligning chairs as the city prepared for lunch, *la hora de la comida*, the time when the tables that were now deserted and naked would be inhabited by congregations of people. Friends, business partners, and *novios* would come together, hands would be held, papers would be signed, new friendships would form, drinks would flow.

This restaurant was where Samantha and Keith had sat for hours, getting to know each other, years before.

It had all been set in motion by a simple phone call.

Keith's phone rang unusually early that Saturday morning all those years ago.

"Keith?" asked a female voice he did not immediately recognize in response to his cheerful greeting.

Since he lived with his girlfriend Norma, an unfamiliar female caller caught Keith off guard so early in the morning. "Yes. Who is this?" he asked tentatively.

"It's Rachel Goetz. Rach, güey."

"Rach, what a surprise!"

Norma walked past mouthing a silent "Who is it?" that Keith casually waved aside.

"Oh, so you remember me?" returned the voice on the phone.

"Believe me, I've tried to forget you, but you keep popping up. Of course I remember you. What's up? It's been a while."

"Well, I've—or rather Charlie, Sam, me, and several other people—have been trying to get ahold of you. Somebody got your mom's number and she gave us yours. Hope that's okay. I lost your cell phone number a few months back. Anyway, a group of us is getting together for lunch and we wanted to see if you'd join us. Olegario—you remember him? He was in school with us, one grade below? Or was he in your class?"

"Tall, skinny guy?"

"That's him. Still looks the same. Anyway, he became a priest a long time ago, but he's being sent to Italy in a few weeks, the Vatican actually, so we thought it would be a good occasion to get our old school group together. It's been so long."

The "so long" she referred to was more than twenty years. A lifetime ago. They'd been little kids back then. He remembered Rachel and Olegario and of course Alberto and Charlie. Above all, he remembered Samantha Riley. Sam. He had not seen her in decades. He remembered her as a lanky, blonde, freckle-faced little girl with blue eyes.

After determining that this was not an invitation for next week or next month but for today, Keith made a quick assessment of his day's activities and agreed to meet at 2:30 sharp at a little restaurant in the downtown square of the small town of his youth. The name of the restaurant sounded familiar. He knew he'd passed in front of it countless times though, he'd never actually been inside.

When Keith told Norma he was going to lunch in Cuernavaca with some old buddies from school, she was a bit surprised, since Keith wasn't a guy who had many friends.

Norma, on the other hand, had spent two years getting her MBA from the University of North Carolina, and she had formed a group of friends that had vowed to stay in touch. Some had kept their promise, and a couple had actually ended up working in Mexico City.

In addition, as a single and very attractive woman working in a foreign country, Norma had immediately begun attending the company-sponsored ex-pat mixers. It was there that she'd been immediately adopted by Becky, or Big Beck, as Keith called her, although not to her face.

Becky was as sweet as she was large. An attractive woman who just happened to be 6'1" in her bare feet and had the build of a linebacker, she wasn't fat, just big. Big bones, big feet, gigantic tits. That was Becky.

Becky had been in this country for almost six years now, and she knew people, places, and things. She taught Norma how to drive the stick shift car the company assigned her and immediately showed her shopping plazas, a hair and nail salon, and all the ins and outs of the huge city. Norma had the advantage over Becky in that she spoke a very passable Spanish.

Keith met Norma at a party hosted by his friend Becky, a colleague at the design firm he worked at. Becky and her Belgian husband Nicholas were great hosts, but in Keith's opinion, this was a very American party, which meant that people mingled, made small talk, drank too little, and remained impeccably and politically correct at all times.

Close to midnight, after chatting with the attractive Norma for the better part of the evening, Keith had asked her if she wanted to go out for a bit longer. She had surprised him by accepting and surprised herself by having a blast with this fun guy who seemed to know his way around areas of the city that everyone had emphatically warned her to stay away from.

They'd eventually landed at a dark and smoky club where a rock band did some decent covers of Lynyrd Skynyrd and the Eagles. Norma was in heaven, surprised that a bunch of local bands could play good ole southern-tinted rock. They both drank and smoked too much and ended at Norma's place where, true to her Southern upbringing, Norma told Keith he could stay in the guest bedroom so he wouldn't have to drive home at this ungodly hour after the impressive quantities of tequila they had consumed.

They woke up sadly hung over, so Keith made eggs and coffee, gave Norma three aspirin, and left her fast asleep. The next day, he called and asked her out. To his surprise, she accepted. After a few more dates, they both experienced a feeling of peace that grew in comfort and intensity. Living in the same area of Mexico City brought them together, and they realized they filled each other with shared moments that felt right, comfortable, warm, and increasingly much more than a friendship. Eventually, Norma invited Keith into her bed.

Soon, Keith was spending more time at Norma's place than his own. Although his apartment was nice, it didn't compare to the splendid duplex Norma lived in. It was part of the compensation package she received at the financial services company that had hired her straight out of grad school five years ago and had sent her to Mexico City.

After a short time, they agreed that Keith would let go of his apartment and move in with Norma. It was a first for both but an easy decision to make. They were seemingly in love, in spite of their differences, and Keith had once or twice broached the subject of marriage and mini-Normas in the not-so-distant future. Norma was thirty and Keith was almost twenty-nine. Years later, he would think of the years with Norma as some of the happiest times of his life.

The morning Rachel called was beautiful. As Keith and Norma sat together on the terrace, sipping coffee and reading the Saturday paper, Norma reminded him they had a party that night and to not get home too late. She also mentioned in passing that he shouldn't drink too much if he were driving on the highway on his way back. She seemed anxious and on edge. Keith was sensing she might have problems at work but thought they could discuss it over a long walk the next day.

"Hey, it's me you're talking to," he said as he poured more coffee.

"I know you're a careful driver even when you drink. Still don't know how you do it. Anyway, I just worry about you."

"Nothing to worry about. This isn't Jay; these are my decent friends. One of them is a priest, for crying out loud! I don't see us drinking until dawn," he assured her.

"Unless your friend Charlie shows up. From what you've told me, he sounds like quite a jewel of a guy," she teased.

"Well, yes, that could change things," Keith conceded. "But I haven't seen him in years. He might be a recovering alcoholic who has found the Lord."

"Honey, your friends will never be recovering alcoholics because they will always simply be alcoholics. The un-repenting kind who never find the Lord."

As he was walking out the door, Norma asked, almost as an after-thought, "Is Alexandra going to be there?"

Alexandra was someone Keith had dated for a few years. She had left Mexico years earlier and had married in Israel. Norma had heard Keith's friends mention her, and she was vaguely concerned that Keith might still feel something for her.

"Norma... Alexandra doesn't live here, and she was never part of this group of friends. We've been together long enough for you to know how much I love you."

"Just checking." Norma hesitated for a moment. "Try to get home early because I want to tell you something..." Her voice trailed off.

"What is it, sweetie?"

"Nothing...Go have fun. We'll talk tonight."

Keith stood up, smiling at the brown arching eyebrows that gave Norma a look of perpetual amazement. He left the table and headed for the shower, where he painted a mental picture of each of his school companions and what they might look like after all these years. Little did he know that, upon his return, a storm would hit that would fracture a relationship he considered a certainty in his life.

The hour-long drive was uneventful. There was no big holiday that day, so the road was nice and quiet. He left early so he could stop by and play some tennis at his parent's home, shower, and head out to the luncheon. With no massive exodus from the capital city spilling out onto the highway, it was a pleasure to drive.

After the initial climb out of the valley, the road traversed through beautiful expanses of land that dipped and rolled into the mountains on the eastern side of the road. These hills led to the Ajusco Mountain and beyond into the neighboring state.

The land was deep green, the cut hay bundled into gigantic rolls that flanked the open prairies. This was a part of the highway Keith had loved since he'd first moved with his parents away from the huge capital city.

He was sure he knew this road like few others did after the countless years he'd traveled it. He knew the dangerous curves ahead, those marked as such and also those that were unmarked and extremely hard to manage at high speeds.

Along with the beauty of the landscape, he remembered the many accidents he'd witnessed over the years by people distracted by the gorgeous scenery or those irresponsible enough to drive after drinking too much.

One accident in particular came to mind. He remembered that rainy night years ago when he'd stopped to help some young kids who had been in a severe wreck. Fortunately, their car had ended up close to the right lane embankment rather than in the middle of the highway where Keith or any other driver would have plowed into it.

Shortly after Keith stopped his car ahead of the crash, one of the young boys ran up, asking to use his cell phone. Keith himself had been drinking, but even in his slow-motion state, he could see the blank and lost look on the boy who reeked of liquor.

As the boy made his call, Keith cautiously walked over to the accident. As he approached the car, he could hear a female voice pleading, "*Ayúdenme. Alguien. Rodrigo, ayúdame! Sácame de aquí!*"

There was no answer to her cries for help.

Peering closer, Keith realized two girls were trapped inside. The body of one of the girls was only halfway inside the car, her hips and legs dangling outside.

All Keith had the courage to do was to gently pull her out and lay her on the wet pavement. He noticed a lot of blood but didn't know where it was coming from. The young woman reeked of liquor and the sweet odd scent of blood.

The other girl was stuck deep in the wreckage. She moaned something Keith couldn't understand before he heard a gasp and then complete silence.

After that, every time he passed that spot, Keith wondered if he'd actually heard the girl die.

Looking around in the dark, he'd noticed a young man standing by himself in the rain, staring into a distant gulf of guilt that would stay with him for a lifetime.

There was so much Keith wanted to tell him. Like how stupid they all were for drinking and driving. He wanted to lash out at their stupidity, at their lack of responsibility, but he was obviously in no position to judge. All he could do was try to help.

Keith felt the decency of a man who wanted to do something, anything, to help, even if it was nothing more than cover them with a blanket as they hurt and moaned. He wanted whatever parent, sister, or brother would weep for them in a gray emergency room to know there had been a moment of warmth, of someone caring for their beloved children as their lives bled away in puddles on the dark pavement.

After a moment, Keith ran back to his car and pulled out two glow-in-the-dark emergency stands. They seemed wildly inappropriate, but his *gringo* sense of duty told him it was important to alert other drivers that something was going on. He didn't want another car slamming into the kids, or into him, for that matter.

After retrieving his cell phone, he jumped in his car and rushed to where the highway patrol and ambulances always parked by the side of the road a few kilometers ahead. As he got closer, he saw a patrol car rushing out with its lights flashing and siren screaming.

Pulling over, he asked the first guy he saw, "Have you been notified of an accident about seven kilometers from here heading south?"

"Yes. The *patrulla* just left to check it."

"It's bad. I just came from there. There's four or five kids in a black Caribe. There's one girl who can't get out. Please get out there or the girls might die. They look badly hurt. *Se dieron un putazo.*"

As the emergency vehicle sped off, Keith resumed his trip to town. By the time he arrived, the rain had softened. He stumbled into one of the bars on the main square where he told the story to a waiter friend who saw his anxiety and poured him drink after drink. When the bar closed, he stumbled to his car.

He woke up in a hotel not knowing how he'd gotten there. It was a fairly decent place, so he knew instantly he hadn't spent the night prowling the streets for hookers and cheap motels on the south exit of the city.

His head pounding, Keith felt an immediate sense of loss for the young kids at the accident scene. He made a mental note to buy the local newspaper to see if there was anything about the crash in it.

Later, after learning that only one car had been involved in the crash, he felt he'd helped. One person had died at the scene and another had died a few hour later. No names were given, as the police were still trying to reach the families.

The brief article seemed inadequate. There were no words to describe the hurt of those poor kids. There were no words either for the enormous pain of the families that were just now finding out that their sisters and daughters, sons and friends, would never be coming home.

Keith witnessed many more accidents over the years, but none moved him like this one.

He drive all these years later was uneventful, and Keith arrived on time at the restaurant. Typically, this was a bad idea for those who lived in this part of the world. People would agree to meet at 2:00 for lunch, knowing full well they wouldn't arrive until somewhere closer to 3:00 or even 4:00.

When he arrived, only two people sat at the table, Olegario and Rachel. Although he knew Olegario was a Catholic priest, it was still somewhat shocking to see the thin, serious, and tall boy he remembered now transformed into a tall, smiling man in a priest's dark clothes and white collar.

Although they'd never been close friends, the two men recognized each other instantly. After embracing, they sat next to each other at the table. Rachel sat across from them with the same earnest demeanor she'd had in childhood.

Keith had seen Rachel here and there over the years. She had actually dated his friend Jay for a few months way back when. Jay had abruptly ended the relationship when he'd sensed Rachel was looking for a more dedicated relationship that would someday lead to marriage and children.

Keith often wondered what would have happened if Jay and Rachel had ended up together. They were both easy-going people, blessed with the peace of mind that comes from knowing your family has tons of money and there will never be any wants. Perhaps, with Rachel, Jay would have found the peace he'd sought all his life but had never found. Who knew?

Gradually, other former classmates arrived, people Keith had not been close to. Questions were politely asked and answered while attempting to find points of shared interest. While various people sipped wine, Keith had a couple of drinks. Additional members of their class arrived, and the table got louder as more drinks were consumed.

Rachel moved to sit beside Keith. Predictably, after a few glasses of wine, she asked about Jay.

Keith told her that Jay was now remarried with a daughter and seemed to have a pretty nice life. A well-known lawyer, he'd made lots of money on some well-publicized cases. That on top of the substantial money and homes he'd inherited from his parents meant he never had to worry about money.

Keith was always amazed at Jay's ability to be so fucking crazy in his personal life and yet so buttoned-up in his professional world. Then again, that was what Jay thought about him, which was probably why they'd been friends for close to twenty years.

With alcohol coursing through her veins, Rachel confessed to Keith that, years after dating Jay, she still had a crush on him.

Keith laughed. Most women did. The guy was charming, extremely wealthy, and good-looking to boot. "I've heard the story before, Rach. Jay has always been a huge hit with the girls. Maybe that's why I became his friend," he joked. In a moment of shared honesty, he added, "I had a bit of a crush on you when we were kids."

Now it was Rachel's turn to laugh. "Keith, we all knew that."

"Really? Was I that obvious?"

"As obvious as I am about liking Jay. But even when we were kids, you always liked Sam more."

"Maybe. Fortunately, that was long ago. Shit, we were just children! And it's too late for all that now. Unfortunately for you, as much as I adore you, Jay's new wife is a hoot and very hot."

"Down, boy! Don't tell me you've got the hots for your best friend's wife?"

"You are too much, my dear Rachel. Of course I don't. She's just hot. Very."

"So, how's Norma? It is Norma, right?" Rachel asked, flirtingly changing the subject.

"She's fine."

"How come you didn't invite her to meet some of your friends? Thought we might embarrass you in front of your girlfriend?"

"You've met Norma several times, but today I thought it would be nice to come alone and just hang out. Plus, she's always super busy."

"So, tell me, is she the one? Is it serious?"

"We've been living together for almost two years now. I'd say it is very serious. I wouldn't mind having my first set of twins with her."

"Oh, so you haven't given up on having a bunch of kids? How do you plan on supporting them?"

"We manage quite well, thank you."

"By the way, Charlie is traveling and won't make it." Rachel abruptly changed the subject. "Samantha might not come after all, either. I'm sure you really came to see her, not me. The story of our lives! She had something with one of her kids. One of them got sick, I think. I don't know if you know, but she has two girls, pretty as can be. Emma and Andrea. One's four and the older one is seven or around there."

"Wow. Two girls, huh? She started young. She's barely thirty." Keith himself was now the ripe old age of thirty-one.

"Well, she married young. She was probably sixteen."

"Holy fuck. That's young even for Mexico. Was she pregnant?"

"No, but everybody thought she was. Proved everyone wrong."

"So, what does she do?"

"Do?"

"Yeah, you know, work? Where did she go to school? Profession? What some of us have to do day in and day out."

"You're kidding, right?"

"Why would I?"

"Sam didn't go to college. No need. Her parents had a lot of money. You knew that. Don't act so surprised. And she married into more money before she finished high school. She and her husband have all kinds of businesses: clothing stores, a couple of car dealerships, a furniture store, and two or three restaurants. I'm sure you've heard of or eaten at Las Azaleas. That's theirs. He runs them. She spends the profits. You might have heard of her husband, Alejandro Alex Cortina. He and his family are well known here in Cuernavaca and in Mexico City. Really nice guy. A bit older than all of us. "

"The name rings a bell. Sounds like a good arrangement for her."

"Well, they seem to be a good couple. Anyway, she works hard, you know, in between the blowjobs and the charity galas and sending her daughters everywhere with the nannies. She's in charge of counting all their millions, cleaning her tiaras, and rearranging the furniture in their mansion. Oh, and shopping, of course. Can't forget shopping!"

"The poor thing," Keith said, but it felt a bit forced.

"Well, believe it or not, money, which she has a lot of, can't buy you happiness. Yet she seems happy."

"Rach, that's what those of us who don't have money say to justify our shitty lives. The reality is that money can definitely buy you happiness. Or something that looks a lot like it. Shit, you should know, your family is loaded."

Rachel's father, Hugo Goetz, was a well-known businessman, owner of some sort of mining enterprise. Keith remembered attending a party at her house when they were young. He had never seen a house like that, except maybe Jay's.

There was a gate before you got to the enormous house with security gurads, *guaruras*, stopping all entering vehicles, standing in their cheap, ill-fitting suits that failed to conceal the guns tucked into their waistbands.

Keith's mother, who was dropping him off, had been shocked to see that type of security. This was long before it became necessary for the very wealthy in Mexico to have such shows of protection.

"True, but I've always worked hard and never took a job with my dad."

"You'll still inherit all his money one day."

"Unless my brothers die, I'll have to share it."

Keith turned to her, forgetting Rachel's dry, hard humor, unsure of whether she was trying to be funny or was just plain mean.

"I'm sure there's plenty to go around."

"True, but in the meantime, I bust my ass at work every single day."

"Stop telling me about all your great virtues, plus all the money you'll inherit, or I'll fall in love with you all over again."

"Liar."

Many of their friends had wondered why Keith and Rachel hadn't ended up together. The fact was, time had never been on their side. Either she was in a relationship or he was, and there was an almost brother and sister feel to their affection for each other, always teasing, always finding a way to one up the other.

Food arrived at their long table, and conversation flowed as a few bottles of wine were passed around. Around 5:00, Keith got up to leave. He was in good spirits, having seen people he hadn't met up with in a while. Although shy by nature, he had been chatty and interested in the lives his childhood friends and classmates now led. They were decent people, mostly well off, with wives, children, and expensive homes. He wondered why exactly he didn't have that kind of life yet, or if he'd ever have it.

As he was saying his farewells, he turned and saw Samantha Riley come into the restaurant. He recognized her instantly.

She approached the group with a smile that seemed genuine, going around the table, kissing everyone and saying hello in a voice that was deep and friendly.

When she got to him, Keith felt himself turn a pale shade of red. There was a bravado in her that perhaps compensated for an innate shyness or self-consciousness. He could see in the woman in front of him the same fine features and long legs of the little girl he remembered from long ago.

"Hi, Keith. You haven't changed a bit," she declared in the gravelly voice he'd come to recognize so well as a kid. She spoke in Spanish with almost no accent.

"Hi, Samantha Riley. You're a lot taller than I remembered."

She laughed and looked him boldly up and down. "You'd better not be leaving, 'cause I came just to hear what you've been up to for the last twenty-some years."

Keith, taken aback by her frankness, did his best to avoid looking into her cleavage, which was deep, stunning, and full of freckles. She had begun speaking in English, their language as children at school, and he noticed that her British accent was much more subdued than it had been in her childhood.

He immediately ordered her a drink and one for himself, and they ended up facing each other at the table. He made a mental note to remember the drink she seemed to enjoy: Absolut and club soda. They sat looking at each other, talking briskly for a few minutes, before Keith had to head back to Mexico City in order to keep his evening plans with Norma.

As he walked out of the restaurant, he felt that odd sense of excitement he'd felt all those years before, standing at school, looking up to the railing above as his friends told him, "That's Samantha Riley."

As he had twenty-two years earlier, he was unable to define what he felt. Back then, he'd run home and told his mother with the unwavering conviction of an eleven-year old boy, "Today I saw the prettiest girl in the whole world."

Today, he couldn't run to his mom, much less to Norma. All the same, he knew he'd think of Samantha on the way home. And he did.

✦✦✦✦✦✦✦✦✦

When he pulled in the driveway, Norma was just arriving with an odd assortment of bags and boxes. He gave her a hand, vaguely wondering what she was doing with all that paraphernalia.

"How was lunch? Did you do a lot of flirting with all your old classmates?" she teased.

Keith noted that she seemed excited and a bit nervous. It must have something to do with the party they were attending that evening at her boss's home.

"Well, not too much," he answered, pretty sure it was the truth.

"How were all your friends?"

"Shit, they're all so old!"

"They? You are too, old man. What about Charlie? I only met him once, but he looks like trouble."

"He couldn't make it. Not sure why."

"Was Rachel there? From the few times I've met her, she seems like a nice girl. The kind of girl you should be running around with."

"Yes."

"Yes, she was there? Or yes, she's the kind of girl you should date?"

"Both," he said in jest. "No, yes, she was there, and no, I shouldn't run around with someone like her. I have you. She asked how you were. Then she asked if we were serious."

"Serious about what?"

"You know...us. You and me. If we were serious."

"And, are we?"

"What do you think?" he laughed. "We live together. We've talked about moving back to the US together. We've talked about having kids. Okay, I've done most of the talking on that subject. You're thirty, I'm twenty-eight. We make a very decent living. We travel together. I think we are serious. Very."

"Yeah, but that doesn't answer the question."

Keith turned and saw a changed expression on her face as they placed bags in the kitchen.

"What do you mean it doesn't answer the question?" He had the slight sense of something beneath the surface that needed to be discussed.

Norma was quiet for a few seconds. When she spoke again, she sounded different. The fun, teasing tone of an instant ago was gone. In fact, she seemed upset, as if anger had been right at the surface of her anxious manner.

"You want the truth?"

"Of course, I want the truth. What's going on?"

"Well, for one thing, I simply can't trust you, Keith. You said you'd be here by 6:00. It's almost 7:00," she blurted, unexpectedly angry.

He looked at her, trying to find a hint of jest. When he found none, he was at a loss.

"What are you talking about? You're just arriving yourself," he responded.

"I just don't see where you want to be in a few years. You talk about kids, about us, about going somewhere. One day it's Budapest; the next day it's New York. One day you want twins; the next you want to fly off to Buenos Aires. I simply don't know. I don't know if I can rely on you. You don't have a definite plan, and I'm not seeing clearly where we're going. I can't live like that."

"Are you fucking kidding me?" Taken completely by surprise, he felt immediate rage.

"Have you been drinking, Keith? You only start cussing when you've been drinking. Jesus, it's only seven, and you're already drunk?"

"What are you talking about? I had a few glasses of wine with my friends. I came home because I knew we'd be going out tonight."

"You are so unreliable. I never know if you'll keep your word."

"What? When have I not kept my word?" He was incredulous. "I do everything I can for you. I'm looking at options at my design firm to move us to the US because it's you who doesn't want to stay here. They have a new office opening in Dallas, and they need someone with my experience. Maybe we can do that? Gets us back to the States. You can surely find a great job in Dallas. "

"Those are your plans. I have my plans too, Keith."

As is often the case when couples argue, things rapidly escalated. Keith was bewildered, and Norma's voice was getting louder.

A pause. A silence. Then Norma blurted, "I have an offer from my company to move."

Keith fumbled for words. He'd known this was a possibility, but he wasn't sure where the moment was taking them. "Well, that's great. It's what you've been saying you want, right? Why didn't you tell me?" he asked, still trying to avert conflict.

"Well, I wasn't sure what I wanted to do. Didn't know how to tell you. I was going to tell you earlier today, but you were too eager to run out and see your friends..."

Her tone was deliberate, hinting at other meanings.

"Where?"

"Where what?" Her words were impatient, as was her manner.

"Well, where are they offering you the job?"

"Egypt."

"Are you kidding? Egypt? Doing what? And what the hell am I supposed to do in Egypt?"

"Well, I'd still be in marketing...and we hadn't discussed you coming."

Immediate silence, a longer silence that crossed the air like an invisible dagger and cut them. She felt pain, and he felt it, too, a second later.

Silence became a physical presence, a living, breathing being that suddenly enveloped the room, stealing their words, coming between them. They were in a dense silence, and the only way out was to argue.

"Oh, so that's what this is about?"

"What?"

"You're getting cold feet. You're backing out. We've been talking about going somewhere together for more than a year. I moved here so we could be together and plan something, and now you have your plan. It was supposed to be *our* plan. You said that. I didn't imagine it, Norma."

"I'm not sure that I'm ready for this, Keith. I feel cornered and pressured by my work, by my parents who don't understand why I'm miles away from them in a dangerous third-world country. And most of all, I feel pressured by you."

"Wait. Back up a second. You're not ready for *what* exactly? Say it!"

"I'm not ready for us to move somewhere together."

"Shit, Norma, we live together. It's a bit late for that."

"Well, maybe we need to go back to each having our own apartment. It might do us some good."

"Are you asking me to move out? Is that what you want? Where is this coming from?" The questions tumbled from Keith's mouth. "Last night in bed you said you loved me. Are those just words that come out of your mouth when you fuck someone? Is that it, Norma?"

"What a shitty thing to say, Keith. I don't have all the goddamn answers. And I've had to put up with your shit for two years, coming home late from God knows where and falling drunk. Give me a break here. I just think we need to give ourselves some time to think things through. I have to make some decisions."

"So now 'I' have to make some decisions. A year ago you wanted me to come live with you. I quit a great fucking job and moved to Mexico. I sold my apartment so we could start something together, have some money to move and buy a bigger, nicer apartment for both of us. I don't know what to say. I can't believe you're doing this to me. To us."

"I'm not doing anything to you. I'm simply telling you that I need time. Please give me that. These are big decisions...Please."

"You know what? I'm off to Jay's place. I think I'll crash there for the night. I'll see you in the morning. Not sure if he's in town, but the guy at the front desk of his apartment will let me in. Won't be the first time..."

"We have the party, Keith. My boss will be there along with the most senior people from work. It's not a huge party, just a few people for dinner, and I already RSVP'd for both of us. They're expecting me to bring someone. They're expecting us."

"Norma, *you* have the party. They're expecting *you*."

"Don't be an asshole, Keith."

"I'm not. You're the one who started this whole argument. I came home looking forward to going out with you. Now it just seems pointless. You need time. Have it. I'll see you in the morning when you make sense. When *we* make sense."

"See what I mean, Keith? I'm talking honestly about what I feel, what I need, and you can't have a decent conversation. You have to run away or attack me. Couples need to talk. That's how it works. And you're way too damn selfish and immature to understand that."

"Clearly, you know a lot about couples. You know so much, Norma, right?"

"All I'm saying is that I have some pretty important decisions to make. It's called growing up, Keith."

"Yeah? Well, part of growing up is also making a fucking commitment to somebody, something you know nothing about. I told you to quit your job, which is really getting to you. You're never home, and you don't seem happy. I told you that I would support you. I meant that. You know I'd do it. You could take some time off."

"Keith, be realistic. You make half of what I make. You really think we could afford this place on your salary alone?" She knew she'd gone to a territory where things could get ugly, but she stood her ground.

"You know what? I think I should leave before we both say things we'll regret." Keith controlled himself with an effort.

"It's a little late for that if you're not coming with me tonight."

"You're crazy. You ask me to leave. You tell me you don't want us to live together anymore. And now you want me to go to a party with you as if nothing happened. Forget it, Norma. Fuck your party! You're absolutely right; you need time, and so do I."

For months after the fight that evening, Keith looked for signs of Norma's unhappiness. He wondered if there was someone else in her life and then discarded the idea. Nonetheless, he wondered how things could have unraveled so quickly. Only years later, with distance and a bit more maturity, could he see that Norma needed someone with a stability that had eluded Keith. He thought of her occasionally over the years, wondering where life had taken her, but concluded their break-up had been for the best.

<hr />

Over the next few weeks, Norma accepted the job in Egypt, and Jay began moving his things out of her apartment. In snatches of conversation here and there, he learned she was going to be in Miami for six months and then on to her new position in Egypt.

Keith had trouble thinking of her without him in a strange country, without speaking the language. In spite of his anger and disappointment, he couldn't help but admire her courage.

He traveled to Miami once to see her, and she traveled to see him in Mexico City a few times, but things had changed. They called each other less frequently, and both felt paralyzed, unable to move the relationship forward. Perhaps a slight effort on the part of either one of them would have inched the relationship to where it could be saved, but neither had the interest or the will.

She called him the day before she left for Egypt and gave him a number where he could reach her. They both cried softly, perhaps waiting for the other to say the words that would bring them together again, but silent tears were all they had to offer.

Keith never called her. He felt angry and betrayed, left behind.

On his birthday, a few months after Norma left, he got a letter from her. She was in Cairo and working her ass off. She missed him but was trying to find some peace after their roller-coaster relationship.

Her exact words.

With the letter, she sent a picture of her sitting on some rocks with the pyramids in the background. She looked as beautiful as always, with her light green eyes and her auburn hair showing under the shade of a hat.

She had remembered that Keith had always talked about visiting the pyramids. On the back of the picture, she'd written:

Keith,

You will one day come and see the pyramids. They are breathtaking. Think of me that day as I thought of you when this picture was taken. Thanks for the great times we shared, and happy birthday, too! Take good care of yourself.

Norma

Chapter 4

About a year later, Keith ran into Rachel Goetz at a bar in Mexico City. Although they spoke on the phone every so often, they hadn't seen each other in some time.

Rachel was with a group of friends, and Keith walked over to say hello before returning to the bar.

After her friends left, Rachel joined Keith. "Need some company, stranger?" she teased as she took the stool beside him.

It was clear she'd been drinking. The deliberate softness in her speech and movements was in sharp contrast to her usual nervous energy.

"I sure do. What's up? Did you chase your friends away? You have to stop doing that. You'll end up a grumpy and lonely old woman."

"Well, I don't see a roaring crowd around you, my friend."

"Ouch."

"So? What's new?"

"Oh, you know, working. Looking around. Having a few... Actually, thinking of moving back to Texas, now that you mention it."

"I don't get that. What's with Texas? Bunch of cowboys in boots and hats and women with hairdos straight out of the seventies. Give me New York, Chicago, DC. Those are cities! Remember when you first came back and we bumped into each other? You were driving down the street over by your parents and I was waiting for a cab. You told me you had just come back from working in Texas. You looked all grown up. You were kind of cute back in the day."

"I still have to fight the ladies off. By the way, you look pretty great tonight. Why are you alone? Where's your last boyfriend you introduced me to? Rafa? Ricky? I know it had an *R*."

"Robby."

"Of course, Robby. How sweet."

"Jealous, my friend?"

"Not really."

"And he most certainly wasn't my boyfriend. I was just using him for sex."

"So, setting aside your sex life for a minute, what else is new?"

"Just out with the girls. They're all rich, married, and need a man to go down on them a.s.a.p. Isn't that sad?"

"That bad?"

"Worse, actually. I guess it's good that we're the single ones. At least I am. Anyway, how've you been? Have you seen Jay?"

"Jay? What about *us*?"

"Boy, are you drunk tonight!"

"What? I thought you were finally going to talk about us and admit we should fly to Las Vegas and get married. Or at least have a fling."

"A fling? Where do you pick up words like that? B movies? And baby, you couldn't afford me."

"I was thinking I could lead a life of leisure with your family's money."

"Sorry, but I'm old fashioned. I don't support men. I just fuck them. So, back to Jay, how is he?

"Had lunch with him a few weeks ago. He's moving back to Spain. Still the same. Still happily married to number two and, unlike your friends, they seem to be doing well."

"Says you. So he's taking his Texan queen to Spain. She is a Texan, right? We'll see how long that lasts! Hopefully a bit longer than his marriage to the Arab girl. I don't see what Jay sees in some of these women."

"He sees..." Keith started to say.

"Pussy?" Rachel chimed in.

"Rachel, Rachel, always to the point!"

"That's me."

"I must admit, I sense jealousy in the air. God, what a little slut you've become."

"Shut up, Miller. I've seen you with at least ten women in the last ten years, so *slut* is more your adjective. You're not exactly the epitome of celibacy. Should be more careful of where you put your *thingy*. You don't want it falling off."

"'Epitome'? Where the hell did you learn such a big word?"

"What? Are you the only one allowed to use big words? I went to Yale, fucker, so there! If I recall correctly, you were always fond of big words like that."

"I know you went to Yale. It's just that your language always comes across as more teamster than Ivy League! That's precisely why I adore you. I've known you for twenty years, and I never know what will come out of that pretty mouth. And I try to be careful with what I say. Besides, I only date virgins, and I'm saving myself for Mrs. Right." He heard himself slur his words a bit.

"I'm sure you are, Keith."

"I haven't had a real date in some time," he admitted.

"Well, you're practically married to Norma. You shouldn't be dating. Right?"

"Well... "

"Well, what?"

"Well, remember when we had the class reunion about eight months ago and you asked me about Norma?'

"Yes. It was a bit over a year ago, by the way, but we digress. How is she?"

"Who?"

"Norma, dumbass."

"Well. She left."

"You said you wanted a woman who traveled, right?"

"No, Rach, she's gone. Completely gone."

"Gone where?"

"Egypt."

"Egypt? So when is she coming back?"

"She's not."

"Oh." There was a long pause while Rachel looked at him. "Oh." The pause grew as Keith's meaning dawned on her.

"I'm sorry Keith, I didn't know," she finally said.

"Well, I guess we were just too different."

"Egypt, huh?"

"Fucking Egypt."

"Talk about chasing people away! At least my exes stay on the same fucking continent!"

They both burst out laughing.

"Truth is, I heard through the grapevine that you and Norma broke up. I got a sense it might not be final. That's why it's so unexpected to hear you say it is."

Keith remained silent for a bit, something Rachel immediately misinterpreted.

"You cheated on her, didn't you? Men just can't keep their dicks in their pants. You motherfucker."

Instead of taking Keith's side, she immediately pounced, establishing her unconditional loyalty to another woman, one she had met no more than three times. Well, why not? They'd only been friends for twenty-some years.

"Rachel, you're supposed to be on my side."

"It's just that men are such losers. Aahhgg. So, did you cheat? Get caught? What was it? Women don't just leave. Men give us reasons."

"And women don't?"

"Rarely."

"No, I didn't cheat. I don't know. It doesn't matter. It just ended, okay?"

"Did you hit her? Did you, you son of a bitch?"

"Of course not. I've never hit a woman in my life."

"Well, maybe you should've hit her. You know that old saying: *Pégame pero no me mates.* It's true. We need a man to take charge sometimes. We say we don't want men to do it, but we really do."

"You crack me up, Rach. When I don't see you for a while, I forget how insane you are."

"You love me anyway."

"I do."

They paused for a moment as Keith lit her cigarette and then his.

"Well, maybe the problem was sexual?" Rachel continued to ponder and probe good-naturedly, quite drunk now.

"Can you just give it a rest?" Keith begged.

"Did you go down on her often?" Rachel took a long swallow of her drink, completely ignoring Keith's question.

"What? You are completely out of your mind! What kind of question is that? I can't believe you just asked that! You're worse than Jay. Shit! You two are so much alike. You should've gotten married twenty years ago."

"Well, I told him so, but what does he do?" Rachel was clearly carrying a torch for Jay. "He goes and marries some...woman. I doubt they could even communicate. She didn't speak Spanish, for the love of God. Or English. Then he married again. That fucker missed out on a great woman."

"Maybe there's a reason you guys didn't make it together, but I still think having my best friends marry each other would have been a good thing."

"You're a sweet guy, Miller, when you want to be. Maybe you should tell Jay that next time you see him. But you're missing the point. Let's get back to your dear Norma...Did you or did you not go down on her every single day? It's a very important question, my dear, innocent, and very male friend. I would not have a man in my life who didn't love going down on me and eating my pussy. Often. And he'd have to be really good. Or a quick learner." She laughed out loud at her own wit.

"I don't think I want to hear about your sexual preferences. I don't want a visual like that haunting me."

"Liar! All men want to know, want to see. Anyway, I guess we'll need some refills to hear the story." She signaled the bartender. Now that her previously slow pace had picked up, she looked perky and inquisitive, as she usually did.

"There is no story." Keith wasn't sure he wanted to talk about it. Nonetheless, when the barman stood in front of them, he went ahead and ordered his tequila neat and a very dry martini for Rachel, even though neither of them needed more alcohol.

"There's always a story," Rachel kept insisting, so Keith gave in and told her about his breakup with Norma. It was a good talk, and the booze helped him become chatty. He actually enjoyed the conversation. He even admitted to Rachel that he missed Norma.

Time passed with the easy conversation between good friends who knew a lot about each other. Keith thought for a second of reaching out to her, of taking her hand, wondering how she'd react. Would they kiss? What would it feel like? Then the thought passed. Rachel was his one good female friend, and he didn't want to screw it up.

After a few minutes of silence, slurring her words, Rachel said, "I know! I'm going to find you a girlfriend!"

"Stop, crazy woman. I can do that on my own."

"And look what happens when you do: they end up in Africa," she teased. "I'm going to find you a really good woman."

Keith paid the bill and they walked outside toward the valet so Rachel could get her car before he went to look for a cab.

As they waited, she blurted, "I know! I'll ask Samantha if she's seeing anyone. She's divorced now, you know."

"Samantha who?"

"Riley. Samantha Riley."

"Samantha Riley?"

"Yes, Keith. Gorgeous woman with legs ten feet long, perfect tits, and a face that should be on the cover of a *Victoria's Secret* catalogue. You went to elementary school with her, and I swear I saw you get a hard-on when she walked into the restaurant at our class reunion. Remember now?" she asked with feigned sarcasm.

"Ohhhh...thaaaaat Samantha," he replied, realizing that the eight tequilas of the night were accomplishing their mission.

"Well, what do you say? I could call her and set it up."

"Let me think about it."

"Have I not taught you anything about women through the years?"

"You mean aside from the importance of going down on them?"

"God! You are such a...pig!"

"Rach, that's exactly what you said."

"It was a metaphor, Keith. A fucking metaphor. God, men just don't get it. No wonder more women are going the lesbian path. Guys are just too stupid."

"Thanks, Rach. Always good to see you, too!"

"You know I love you. Even if you are a guy!"

As she boarded her car and tipped the valet, she rolled down her window and yelled, "I'll tell Samantha you asked about her and that you still like her!"

"How would you know?"

"Pleeeaaase. It's me you're talking to, Mister."

"You shouldn't drive, Rach. I'll drive you home."

"You are such a boy scout. No wonder we never married. I love bad boys who mistreat me, although it is kind of sweet to have someone worry about you for a change. Plus, if you took me home we'd probably end up in bed...Ooops, I said it..."

"C'mon, Rach, let me drive you home. You've had too much to drink."

"Nice offer, Miller, but I must decline. I'm off! And I will tell Samantha you're single again." With those parting words, she sped off, closely missing the car parked beside her.

Behind her, a white Chrysler without plates, carrying three heavyset men, immediately sped away. Keith knew those had to be her bodyguards, and his guilt for not insisting on driving her home immediately vanished.

Standing alone, he blushed, thinking of Samantha Riley. As he flagged a cab, he said out loud, "Shit, what grade are we in? Fifth? But Rach is right, come to think of it. Samantha does have great tits." He smiled to himself as he spilled onto the backseat of the green VW cab.

"*A dónde lo llevo, joven?*" ("Where to?")

"*Pues a buscar al amor de mi vida.*" ("To look for the love of my life.")

"*Uy jovenazo, eso sí que está cabrón,*" ("That's a tough one, young man.")

The cab driver sped off into the night, running the first light they came to, not really giving a flying fuck about the car that honked loudly at the intersection, barely missing them.

Keith ended up asking the cab driver to drop him at his favorite dive. The place had no name and was always open. It was dark and seedy, and once he was inside, Keith felt at home.

The bartender waved hello as Keith staggered in. A woman immediately approached him to bum a cigarette.

Keith lit one for her and was lighting his own when, without preamble, she asked, "Are you looking for the love of your life, handsome?"

"As a matter of fact, I am."

"You've come to the right place," she whispered. "I'm Iris. I've seen you before."

"I've seen you too, *mi vida*. I'm Keith."

"*Kid?*"

"Keith." He tried to say it slowly even though he knew, after all these years in Mexico, his name remained impossible to say in Spanish. "*Keed,*" he told her, giving up.

"Will you buy me a drink?" she asked unctuously.

"Anything you want," he answered, knowing the game.

"Anything, really?" she giggled.

"Anything," he assured her as he placed his drink on the bar.

"You look like a good guy, *Keed*. Buy me that drink, and we'll see where the night takes us."

Chapter 5

Rachel unexpectedly called him up a few months after their drunken encounter at the bar.

"Guess what?" she blurted as soon as he picked up his cell.

"What, my dear Rach?"

"You aren't going to believe it."

"Spit it out, Rachel."

"She said *yes*."

"*Who* said yes?"

"Samantha. She's expecting your call."

"Rach, you shouldn't have."

"What are you talking about? You're both my friends, you're both single, and you're both good people. Plus, I saw the lascivious looks going on last time you guys were together."

"I did not give Samantha any lascivious looks, Rach. I was very decent."

"I was talking about her!"

They laughed as they had laughed for years at the always inappropriate and unexpected comments Rachel came up with.

"I'm not sure this is a good idea, Rach."

"Don't be such a chicken shit, Miller. I spoke to her, and she truly sounded up for it. If it doesn't work out, so what? I did my best for two dear friends. *No pasa nada.* And if it does work out, you can both thank me years from now when you have three pairs of twins and a bunch of Mexican nannies following you around."

"Hold your horses, Rach. Why don't we think this through?"

"Nothing to think about, Miller. You've always liked kids. Here's your chance. She's got two kids. They aren't twins, but they're great kids. Your ready-made family is waiting."

"Wait...listen, why don't we go out. Like on a date."

"That's the point. Are you playing dumb? You're not good at it, Keith."

"No, Rach, you and me."

She laughed lightly and then stopped. "You're asking me out?"

"Yes. Now look who's playing dumb."

"*You and me*? Are you kidding?"

"Why is that so hard to imagine? We've been friends for twenty-five years. We know things about each other that nobody else knows. And nobody *should* know. We could be like the guys in *When Harry Met Sally*. You saw that, didn't you? We know everything about each other. We've been through thick and thin. There would be no surprises. I've seen you pee, I've seen you puke, I've heard you snore..."

"Keith, ten years ago, maybe. Five? Maybe. Not now. We were meant to be friends. Good friends. Why screw things up?"

"Why not try to be more than friends?"

"Look, Keith, I'm flattered. I really am...but it doesn't work that way. Remember the day at the restaurant when we all got together over a year ago? Or even when we were kids at school? Do you remember?"

"Of course I do."

"When Sam finally arrived at the restaurant, I saw you look at her. I saw you look at her as you left. Even when we were kids, I still remember you looking at her when you thought no one was watching. After not seeing her for more than twenty years, you looked at her just as you did back then. We've known each other since sixth grade, right?"

"Right. What's your point?"

"Don't you see it, Keith?" A slight pause. "You've never looked at me that way. Ever."

There wasn't a word on the phone line for a few seconds.

"Keith?

"I'm here...I just..."

"Don't apologize. It is what it is. We're great friends and probably will be until we're old and wrinkled. Unless you piss me off..."

"I...It just doesn't...I don't want to get my heart broken again, Rach."

"Just take it slowly, Keith."

"I still don't know..."

"Don't do this to me, Keith," Rachel interrupted. "I already told her you'd call. Grab a piece of paper and write down her fucking number. Jesus! No wonder you don't have a girlfriend!" she commented good-naturedly.

Keith fumbled for a pen and paper as Rachel gave him the number.

"Got it?"

"Got it."

"Don't fuck it up, Miller. She's a good girl," she told Keith before hanging up.

Keith was wearing jeans, boots impeccable in their luster, a white shirt, and a pale brownish sports coat.

She was stunning in a yellow dress just tight enough to insinuate the soft curves of her waist and bosom and short enough to reveal a good portion of long, well-toned legs with skin a slightly burnt maple.

When Keith arrived at the restaurant, Samantha was already there. He saw her smile and the eyes that shone and twinkled in flashes of blue.

There was eagerness in her dialogue, a combination of mischief, innocence, and awe that unbalanced Keith, that moved him, enveloped him.

The afternoon flew as the questions and answers went back and forth. They revisited their past, revealed personal details, and laughed over memories of friends from long ago.

Keith suddenly realized that Samantha's distinct accent had faded over the years. When he mentioned it, she explained that most of her classmates and friends were American and that she'd spent a year and a half in California during high school where she'd gradually shed most of what remained.

The minute threads that are woven into a shared fabric from which a story evolves were entwined that afternoon. The liquid catalysts of vodka and tequila also helped the afternoon move along and grow in candor.

Samantha drank vodka with uncommon gusto; Keith sipped tequila like it was his story-telling fuel. The alcohol burned their stories with intensity, emotion, and connections that were powerful and confusing at the same time.

They went from the trivia of movies and songs to serious conversations about past relationships, mistakes, regrets, and long-dreamt-of places to visit around the world. They talked about their motivations to leave what seemed like solid, stable relationships and pursue dreams that seemed beautiful yet intangible and even a bit immature.

When Samantha spoke of her daughters, Keith was enthralled. She became a different person. Her brightness continued but it came not from her impeccable attire and her chiseled features but from somewhere warm and untouchable inside. He wanted to be part of that space, to find the core of sun she instantly became.

As they waited for another round of drinks, Keith was transported to that warm afternoon when they had waited outside of school for Sam to be picked up nearly twenty-two years before.

He had gotten rides with her once or twice with the driver who came to pick her up every day at three o'clock sharp. Those brief moments in that old yellow Mercedes had always seemed insufficiently long to allow them to learn much about each other, but still they'd sat together in the back seat, close to each other, not daring to look into each other's eyes, but allowing slight touches of their arms or hands as the car moved through the curls of the city's streets.

That day, as he saw the unmistakable yellow car racing toward them down the deep incline, something kindled a sense of urgency that gave Keith the courage to turn, face Sam, and kiss her.

He could smell the candy on her breath as she turned bright red, bringing her hands to her cheeks. For a moment, Keith thought she might slap him or push him onto the street or both.

An instant before the car came to a stop in front of them, Sam offered Keith one of those little miracles that occur maybe once in a lifetime: she leaned forward and kissed him back, smack on the lips, and said, "I like being your girlfriend."

She quickly turned and got in the car. As it raced off, he could see her in the back window, smiling. Then she waved, and his heart beat faster as he stood speechless in the middle of the street.

That same voice several decades later brought him to the present. Their first afternoon together became night, and still they were deep in conversation.

"So, where would you like to go?" she asked after they'd had dessert and yet another round of drinks.

"We could walk a bit," he said.

They took his car, and he drove toward the place he knew best. The downtown streets of their hometown were packed as rain began to pound. People were running in the middle of the street, trying to find cover.

With their plans for a casual stroll out of the question, they wandered into a dark little café from which the soothing sounds of Silvio Rodriguez's music emanated. Keith knew the song well:

Ojalá pase algo que te borre de pronto:

una luz cegadora, un disparo de nieve.

Ojalá por lo menos que me lleve la muerte.

I hope something happens that erases you forever:

A blinding light, an explosion of snow.

I hope at least death takes you away.

He hummed along for a moment and thought of the many times this song had given him a sense of understanding. It had confirmed to Keith that others also wanted to find refuge from memories that followed them relentlessly.

He turned to see Sam watching him.

"I remember you often spoke of music and of playing. Did you?" she softly asked.

"I did. Played with a few bands. I was never very good, but I had way too much fun. Still play the guitar a bit. I kind of started collecting them a few years back," Keith told her.

They sat for another hour speaking intensely one minute and enjoying the music and the powerful sounds of the rain and thunder the next. The nervousness of the first few hours had passed, and there was now a comfort between them that they both silently assessed and found reassuring. Samantha smiled more easily now, and Keith's constant anxiety had given way, allowing more cadence to his words.

"Remember when we were little?" he asked, secretly hoping she would reveal that she too had kept fragments of those far-away ribbons of time.

"Most of it...Remember that day outside of school? The day you kissed me? What were we? Ten? Eleven?" she asked, smiling openly.

"Samantha, of course I do. But I think it was you who kissed me."

"Dream on, Keith. You practically forced yourself on me."

"Please. I didn't even know how."

"You clearly have memory issues."

"I have issues, but not memory issues. I remember things you wouldn't believe. I have dreamed about that day and relived it countless times. I wanted that brief moment to never end. And you didn't only *try* to kiss me. You got me right on the mouth."

"I did not! Or did I? Wow! Okay, I admit it! I guess I didn't want to forget it, either...but you started it."

Keith immediately saw her again at age ten, skinny, with a look of mischief dancing in her eyes.

Suddenly it was like they were both kids again, ten and twelve, finding a way to navigate the awkwardness and excitement of the moment.

"We had a lot of great times together, playing soccer, swimming at Charlie's, dancing, playing Spin the Bottle," he reminisced.

"Remember that first party at Lety's house?" she smiled warmly.

"Jesus. I even remember your orange dress."

"Orange dress? What orange...? Holy shit! What a memory, Keith Miller! I'm impressed. So you were paying attention."

"You have no idea."

"I had completely forgotten about that dress. My dad brought it from Harrods on one of his trips back home," she reminisced. "Funny how after thirty years of not living there, he always called England home."

"You were hard to miss in that dress... You were hard to miss always," Keith found himself saying.

She lowered her gaze, and a brief moment of silence passed through them. Again they smiled at each other.

"And then one day we were off to different schools." She let the words hang between them.

"It's like we went to different planets." Keith immediately traveled back in time as if to reclaim the regrets of their youth. "How come you never really left this town?" he asked, truly interested. "Even as a kid, I sensed it was too little for you."

She seemed too worldly for Cuernavaca, as if her beauty belonged in LA or Milan. As far as he was concerned, Cuernavaca was just another crowded city with traffic everywhere and the same old orange buses throwing stacks of smoke on the people walking the equally congested sidewalks.

"I was too scared to leave," she confessed. "I'd been here since I was six or seven. This was home. And right before finishing high school, I met Alex. He was everything I thought I wanted in a guy. Or everything an immature sixteen-year-old girl thinks she needs in a guy. I fell in love. My parents adored him. Sure, my dad thought of sending me off to school somewhere in England, but I didn't even consider the possibility. Rather than fight me, they let me marry him. The fact that he was very wealthy probably weighed in. They knew I'd be well taken care of. Or at least I imagine they thought that."

Suddenly, behind this poised woman in her yellow Cavalli dress and the Jimmy Choos casually slung on her feet, was a scared little girl hiding in the shadows of an uncertainty she'd never faced and from which she'd always been sheltered.

"This was the place for me," Sam shrugged. "This was where I married my husband. Ex-husband. And this was where my girls were born, literally five blocks from here at the Hospital Metropolitano. Truth be told, this city has given me a great life. I can't complain, Keith."

For a second, it was her turn to be lost in thought, in a distant moment, a memory traveling at great speed and connecting with her soul for a moment. Then she continued, "Let me ask you, how come you left, Keith? Why do some people always think that those who stay are the ones who lost out on life? What's wrong with staying?"

"I never set out to leave. It just happened. And I never said you lost out on anything. I'm not one to judge." Keith stumbled through his thoughts. "I looked everywhere, and one day I realized...I wasn't sure what I was looking for in the first place. So I moved about. I just wanted to see more of this world. Life happened, Sam. And it often doesn't ask for permission."

"And now?"

"Now I'm back, back in the town I grew up in and sitting here with the girl who stole my heart all those years ago. It feels good to see you, to be sitting here after all this time, in this place where we both grew up."

"I'm sure you tell that to all the girls. Some probably fall for it," she teased.

"Sam, I've told many girls many things, but none of them left the imprint you did. Maybe you didn't know it, but you did."

"An imprint? What do you mean?"

"I mean a mark. Memories. Possibilities."

They both sat quietly for a minute.

"What are you thinking?" Sam asked.

"That I'll soon leave again," Keith admitted. "I've asked the company I work for if I can be relocated to the States. I'm also looking into other options. It's going to take some time."

"Where?"

"Where...?"

"Where do you want to go?"

"Anywhere, I guess. I'm just tired of Mexico. I need a change. How about you?"

"I simply don't know. I was married for so many years that I don't know what living on my own is like. I've never done it. I've always had someone with me: my dad, Alex... That's my soon-to-be ex-husband."

"Oh! I thought you had divorced."

"Just a few more weeks. But we've been separated now for more than a year," she clarified.

"Well...and what's next for you?"

"Now it's just my daughters and me. It's a little scary. A lot scary, to be honest."

"So, what about your marriage? What happened?" Keith wasn't sure he wanted to hear the answers, but the beautiful woman with the smile that never ended endlessly intrigued him.

"I don't know for sure. Jesus, I loved my husband. I had two children with him. We went through so much together. The ups and downs of any relationship. We always managed to come out on top. The money helped I guess. Until it didn't. Don't get me wrong, I know money doesn't make happiness, but it was one worry we didn't have." She was careful with her words, still reserved. "I guess everyday life has a way of chipping away at love and dreams. There's no single answer that encompasses it all. He's a good man, a good father. Sometimes you ask yourself, *is this it? Is this what it's all about? Is this where it starts and it ends?* I'm sure he was asking himself the same questions."

She picked up her glass, looked at him, perhaps asking without words if he was truly interested. She shrugged again. "So now I'm starting again and a bit unclear on more than a few fronts. What I do know is that my girls are my priority, and I will keep them well grounded and protected."

"I think you will enjoy this new period in life. Enjoy your freedom and enjoy your daughters. Rachel told me they're beautiful girls."

"I'm their mom. I might be a little prejudiced, but yes, they are wonderful girls. Andrea is eight and Emma is five," she said, pulling out her wallet to show him a few pictures.

Keith tried to find the resemblance of the girls to their mother but failed to do so. When he saw a family picture of Sam, her girls, and someone he assumed was her ex-husband, the resemblance appeared. The girls looked a lot like their father. For a moment, he felt oddly uncomfortable and a bit jealous.

"How come you don't have kids?" Sam asked. "You mentioned at the luncheon that you really like kids."

"I don't know. Believe me, I've asked myself that question, because I do love children. Especially girls."

"If I recall, you always did like girls," she teased.

"No, that's not what I meant. I mean girls...little girls."

"Okay... that's sounding weirder and weirder by the minute," she teased.

"You know what I mean. I guess I've always wanted a daughter."

"Now you're just trying to be nice to me. First of all, single guys don't like kids. And if they do, they want a son they can dress in their favorite sports team's outfit and wrestle. Then they can't wait to get them drunk when they're fifteen and take them to some topless bar, right? It's okay, you can tell me the truth."

"That definitely sounds like fun, but I just like girls better. I have no idea why."

"Well, I wish I'd had a son. I know my ex would have killed to have a son. We tried. Maybe if we had, we'd still be married."

"There's still time."

"Are you kidding me? I have two daughters and I'm done. Case closed."

"Hey, maybe you'll meet the right guy and change your mind."

"Keith, as hopeless a romantic as I am, I'm done having kids. Been there, done that. And I'm very happy with my girls. But you certainly can have kids. You should. It changes you."

"How?" he asked with genuine interest.

She looked at him for a moment, trying to understand the real question being posed. "It gives you a tremendous sense of responsibility. But as hard as it can be at times, there is no joy that compares to seeing them grow and discover and learn. They need you all the time. And humans need to feel needed. We do, don't we?"

"I agree."

"How come you're not married?" she continued to press. "Mid-thirties, handsome, doing well for yourself, it seems."

"I don't know. I scare the good ones away." He looked away, feeling terribly self-conscious talking about himself and his love life. "I came close once," he admitted after a pause.

"Rachel told me about your girlfriend moving away. Was that your close encounter with marriage? Did you run from commitment?"

"Actually, I didn't. I think Norma—that was her name—was the one who ran. There was a time when I felt sure we had a great future together: kids, house with a white picket fence, the works. I guess we were both too selfish. Or maybe I was too selfish and she was too independent. I don't know."

"Are you still in touch with her?" Sam asked cautiously.

"No," he answered. "We've moved on. She's living in Egypt last I heard."

"Really? Egypt? That's pretty far to run from a guy," Sam blurted.

Keith laughed openly at her remark.

"Sorry. That came out wrong." Sam laughed, too. "I am so, *so* sorry."

"It did come out wrong, but it's kind of funny. Rachel made the same comment, in her own words, of course."

"She does have a way of blurting out some really crude comments, that sweet friend of ours."

"She's funny as hell, though. Anyway, it's all in the past now."

"Do you still miss her?"

Keith had not expected Samantha to ask that, and he felt himself hesitate again. "I did, of course. Now, more than missing her, I think I sometimes find myself thinking what it could have been like to stay together. It's like you don't miss the person but you miss the possibilities, the what if's. Does that make sense?"

"I'm not sure. Either you miss someone or you don't. Or you are beginning to not miss them. The problem is that sometimes when you miss someone, that someone is just running away and doesn't miss you back."

He paused a minute and took a sip of the strong coffee. "I don't think she was running from me as much as she was running from herself."

"I guess we all have our own ghosts to run away from."

They went back to enjoying the rain, but after a few minutes, Sam looked at her watch.

"It's getting late. I think you should take me to my car."

"Are you sure?"

"Not really," she said softly. "But I think it's best."

They walked briskly, trying to avoid getting soaked, but by the time they reached Keith's car, they were completely drenched.

He pulled some tissues out of the console to dry their faces and clear his glasses.

Once they reached her parked car, he offered to follow her home.

"No need, Keith, but thanks anyway."

"It was so nice talking to you, spending time together. Like I said earlier, changing schools was like changing planets. I often wondered what became of you," Keith admitted. "What you looked like. Who you became. Maybe I can see you if you're in the city sometime. We can have dinner."

"Maybe," she said casually, evasively, as she looked in her purse for her keys.

"At least let me call you. Don't answer now, you can think about it. You have my card."

"I think we need time. I need time."

"Well, good night, Samantha."

"Good night." Getting out of his car, she hesitated. "I want to be honest with you, Keith."

"I'd appreciate that. You'll get nothing but honesty in return."

"I'm in a strange place right now. I'm not sure where I'm going. I'm not sure who I am. And I'm not sure why I'm telling you this. But there it is." She blushed a bit as he gazed into her blue eyes.

"It was good to see you today, Keith," she added. "I didn't know what to expect, and I had a great time. I think I drank too much. I'm sorry."

"Hey, I had a few drinks, too. We've been pretty good. Are you sure you can drive?"

"Yeah. The coffee helped. I never drink coffee. I'll probably be awake until Sunday!"

She laughed, and Keith was in awe of the sound.

"I'll say it again, Sam...I had such a good time. It's been a while... so, think about getting together again."

She paused. "I'm not really sure what everything I just told you means, but I thought you should know."

She stepped out of the car into the pouring rain but seemed unable to end the conversation.

After a pause, dripping anew, she sat down again and pulled the door closed. "All this is new for me."

For a brief moment, Keith thought she might cry. "You're not alone, Samantha. Hell, there are days when I don't know who I am either. Where I'm going. It happens. That's why it's time for me to move back to the States."

"You're pretty set on that, aren't you?" she asked point blank.

"I am, Sam. It's time."

"Well, I'm sure you'll do well, wherever you go. You'll settle down, find a wife, and have children. There's nothing wrong with that."

"I never said there was. Actually, I'd like that."

"Just keep your eyes open."

"I have my eyes open this very instant. I really hope to see you again, Sam."

"I have to go."

"Don't go yet."

"I have to. My girls are waiting up for me."

After kissing Keith lightly on the cheek, she got out of the car.

Helpless to stop himself, Keith got out, too. He cupped his hands to his mouth, standing by his car, with his coat still draped over him to protect him from the pouring rain.

He was just getting into his car when she backed up. Rolling down her window, she yelled through the rain that was suddenly heavy and loud again, "Okay!"

"Okay what?" He cupped his hands to his mouth, standing by his car, still covering himself with his coat from the pouring rain.

"Dinner! Next Saturday. Call me!" she yelled and then immediately drove off.

A few days later, Samantha received some flowers. She didn't have to open the card to know they were from Keith.

That night, after tucking the girls into bed, she took the note that had arrived with the flowers and read it again. *"I'm enjoying seeing the girl of my dreams become such a charming and wonderful woman."*

For some strange reason, she imagined he had been waiting a long time to write those words in that small, typewritten note. It was brief but deliberately written. A small *K* was all he'd signed. She smiled to herself in the humid night air.

Chapter 6

They did see each other again.

After dating for several months, Keith and Sam finally wondered to themselves where their encounters were taking them. They had very tenuously touched on the complexities of a life together with Sam's children even as their affection and profound sense that they belonged to one another grew with each new encounter.

They were moving forward with nothing but their mutual will as a guideline when Keith met Emma and Andrea, the two beautiful girls from Sam's first marriage. By the time Sam and the girls boarded a plane to move north to Texas along with their shared possessions, Keith had fallen under the girls' spell just as he had fallen under Sam's.

Andrea was nine years old with a tenderness and innocence that only the firstborn can possess. Her eyes were pools of trust and adoration for her mom, her dad, and her younger sister, but her parents' divorce weighed on her, and she had retreated into long spells of silence and the relentless quest to find happiness in a place that wasn't home. In response, Sam filled her afternoons with activities and an endless stream of friends as if afraid of leaving Andrea alone with her sadness.

Andrea looked upon Keith's presence around her mother with mild fear and the natural but guarded curiosity of a young girl. She wanted to like Keith, but letting affection come into play felt like an act of disloyalty to her father, whom she idolized.

Finally, her father's growing absence allowed Andrea's affection to evolve into admiration toward this strange man her mother had attached herself to. She sensed an understanding from Keith that was new to her. Both her mother and father had well-defined expectations of what she should do, how she should behave, and what she should be, but as long as she did her best, Keith let her find her way. He was ever patient in contrast to Sam's perpetual sense of urgency.

But as time went by, Andrea sensed that she had to constantly meet his expectations. She sometimes felt that she wasn't quite good enough in Keith's eyes, whether she was competing in gymnastics or earning grades at school. He was adamant about high grades, and Andrea didn't always feel the same way. And so, over the years, she and Keith played a balancing game of give and take. He almost always returned from business trips with a little surprise for her and Emma, but sometimes there was an unexpected burst of anger that scared her, sometimes for a chore not done or homework not completed or a grade that he didn't approve of.

In due time though, Andrea and Keith learned to love each other. Deeply.

Emma, on the other hand, simply strolled into Keith's life and stole his heart.

She was all of five years old when she and Keith first met. He and Sam had been dating for a few months when she asked if he would like to meet her younger daughter, since he'd met Andrea when dropping Sam off one evening after Emma was already in bed.

Keith had looked forward to meeting Sam's second daughter but was totally unprepared for the smart, eloquent, and curious child who came down the stairs that afternoon with a sparkle in her blue eyes.

As soon as she saw him, Emma turned to her mother and said, "Mom, you said he was really nice. He looks too serious." She walked up to Keith and continued, "Hi, I'm Emma, but my daddy and my mommy call me Emmy. You can call me that, too. Do you always wear glasses? Is that your car parked outside? Why is it white? Doesn't it get dirty when it rains? I know rain comes from the clouds. My teacher taught me that. Her name is Miss Rosario."

"Yes, I wear them most of the time," Keith replied, trying to process her incessant questions. "It's very nice meeting you. I'm Keith."

"I know *that*. My mom showed me a picture of you. What I don't know is if you can fix my bike. The chain fell off. Can you? Will you? C'mon, let me show you."

Sam tried to contain the child's barrage of questions and requests, but Keith was delighted with this little girl who, much to his surprise, shared his light brown skin and toothy smile.

She instantly took his hand and pulled him to the backyard where her bike leaned against a chair. Keith looked at Sam standing against the screen door. She smiled as Emma continued her endless chatter.

"Do you think you can fix it? My daddy can. He's really smart. Can you?"

Before Keith could answer, Emma continued, "Well? Can you? And how come your jeans have holes in the *pompis*?" she giggled, inspecting the tattered backside of his jeans.

Watching them interact, Sam breathed deeply with relief, knowing Emma would be okay with Keith coming into their lives. As for Andrea, she wasn't yet sure.

That night, Sam called Keith to make sure he had made it safely back into the city. His phone at home rang just a few minutes after he walked in the door.

"Hello?"

"It's me."

"Just coming in the door."

"Well, you were quite a hit with Emma. She asked if you were visiting again...even if you weren't able to fix her bike!"

"I tried, I swear."

"You'll get the hang of it...but you might want to consider wearing jeans with no holes in the butt next time. Emma just blurted out to her father a while ago on the phone, "I could see mommy's friend's underwear through the holes in his jeans."

"Oh, boy!"

"We don't want anyone thinking you're some pervert. Least of all my ex."

"I'll explain when I meet him."

Silence.

"You know it's going to happen sometime."

"Meeting Alex? I'm sure it will happen, but I'd rather wait twenty years or so." Sam laughed lightly at her remark.

"Me too... Emma's an adorable child, Sam. I'm glad I met her, finally. And so is Andrea, of course. You're very lucky."

"I just wanted to say thank you for being so patient with the girls. They'll get used to you. Andrea might take a bit longer. I know she misses her dad."

"I can wait."

Keith continued to think his immediate future would take him back to the US. He had traveled twice to interview with a leading graphic design company in Dallas, a small firm with an enviable list of clients, while Samantha continued to adjust to living outside her recently ended marriage with the sole responsibility of raising her daughters and profound uncertainties of her own.

In December of that year, she took the girls to Dallas. Her sister Rose lived there, and her parents were visiting for the holidays. After twenty years in Mexico, they'd moved back to the UK, though they kept a small home in Cuernavaca that they visited less and less frequently as they got older.

Before she left, Keith mentioned a job opportunity that had just arisen in Dallas. Sam took it in stride, as she and Keith both felt it was premature to make any decisions about their relationship.

There was an easy, comfortable feeling between them. It was the period in all relationships when questions are asked with hope, when opinions are exchanged seeking acquiescence, when tentative steps toward deeper intimacy are taken. Although Keith and Sam were clearly falling in love, neither had come out and irrefutably said it out loud. It was a tangible matter waiting to be bravely and frankly addressed.

Sam called Keith from Dallas the first day of the new year.

"Happy New Year, Keith," she spoke merrily into the phone.

"Happy New Year, Sammy."

"You've never called me that before. That's what my dad called me when I was little. Long time ago."

"It just came out."

"I like it."

"Have you had a chance to miss me a bit?" he asked, enjoying their conversation.

"I have." After a brief hesitation, she continued, "I told my parents about you. About us."

"Oh." Pause. "And?"

"They remember you from school."

"That can't be good. I wasn't always the model student."

"They think they met your parents years ago."

"My mom thinks so too, remember? I'm sure they had tons of friends in common. Cuernavaca was a really small town back then. Everyone knew everyone. Anyway, go on."

"They think it's too soon after the separation for me to get involved with anyone. They worry about the girls. They are my parents, Keith. They mean well, but..."

"Sounds like they aren't thrilled. You can tell me. I'm a big boy."

"It's nothing specific about *you*. I think they still hope that Alex and I will get back together. I told them that's not a possibility, that the marriage is over. They want Alex and me to do the right thing. They want me to take time to sort things out. And they don't want Andrea and Emma getting hurt. I think that's their main concern, and I understand that."

"We've done things right, Sam. You've always had the girls' best interests at heart. I'm learning about them, and they're learning about this guy who's suddenly in their lives. I know I don't know much about kids, but I'm learning."

"It takes time, Keith. You've been patient, and I need you to be even more patient."

"I can do that, Sam. As long as you aren't giving up on us. You aren't, are you?"

"Of course not. Let's just take our time. It's only been a few months, and I want this to work. I want *us* to work."

"I want us to work too. This time apart will help us think things through. At least it will help me," he added.

"I have to go, Keith. My sister and my parents are up."

"How are the girls?"

"They're having a blast! Emma asked 'Are Keith and Daddy coming soon?' I almost had a heart attack in front of my parents! She's so little she doesn't understand. You have to admit, it was pretty adorable. Andrea was mortified. *She* understands."

"I'm sure your parents were horrified."

"Pretty much...Anyway, I'll be back soon. I hope you can pick us up at the airport."

"I'll be there. I miss you, Sam. A lot."

"Gotta go. I miss you too."

As he put the phone down, he heard her say for the first time, "I love you, Keith."

Before he could say anything, she had hung up.

As their relationship deepened, Keith learned that Sam showed her love in brief and unexpected bursts of enthusiasm.

Upon her return from Dallas, their constellation of shared moments led them to believe that *this* was what they had been looking for their entire lives. They were falling in love, and they both felt this was a chance they couldn't pass up.

Life had finally reunited them after their brief encounter as children and now offered them the natural answer to the childish, wishful thinking of years ago. In an instant that could never be truly identified or captured, they made the unspoken commitment to build a life together.

Five months later, when Keith was offered a position with the Dallas design firm, he accepted. It was the right move, professionally and personally, although he was unsure of Sam's reaction to this significant piece of information.

But Sam managed to surprise him once again. With the easy and innocent candor she exuded, she smiled and said, "I knew you'd get it. The girls and I are going with you. Isn't that great?"

Keith was speechless. After a few seconds he managed to ask her, "Are you sure?"

"Of course I'm sure. I mentioned it to my ex. As long as it doesn't cost him a cent, he'll be okay. I told him the girls will be fine. Alex knows my sister lives there."

The following few months were a whirlwind of activity. Keith moved to Dallas and started his new job while Sam threw herself into the packing and inventorying that was required for a full house with all its contents to be shipped to another country.

He'd arrive home late in the evening and call her. Invariably, she'd yell into the phone, "Dallas, here we come!"

The girls were uncertain, worried about leaving their father, but slowly they accepted the idea. That summer, after moving to Dallas, they began settling into their new suburban life and making friends in the neighborhood. Initially, they spoke to their dad frequently, but eventually their relationship was sustained with nothing more than minimal calls and the occasional visit.

In spite of the pressures of his new job, Keith made sure he was always available for the three women in his life.

"Are you happy with me, Keith?" Sam sometimes asked. "Please tell me this isn't just a dream."

"It's not, Sam. We waited long enough for this to happen. We're together in Texas. I love it here with you and the girls."

Some months later, holding each other in bed one evening, Keith broached the topic most near and dear to his heart.

"I think we should get married. It would be better for the girls. I want Andrea and Emma to know we're doing things right and for the right reasons."

"Are you asking me to marry you, Keith Miller?"

"I think I just did, Sam. I am...Will you? Will you marry me?"

In the darkness, she hugged him fiercely and began to cry. "Of course I will, Keith. Of course I will."

"Are you sure? Shouldn't you be happy instead of crying?"

"I'm crying because I *am* happy."

Keith held her in his arms for a long time until she dropped off to sleep, in heaven that she had agreed to marry him, relieved that she was happy and excited in their new home. She was a free spirit, a free soul, and a source of constant amazement to Keith.

Their wedding was a very simple affair. Thirty people at most, parents and siblings, close friends, and a sprinkling of odd characters. In its simplicity, Keith often wondered if the ceremony lacked substance, if a more elaborate ritual would have felt more meaningful. In hindsight, he couldn't help but feel it lacked splendor, even though the wedding of that boy and that girl turned into a memorable affair for his family, who had taken an immediate liking to Samantha and her girls and had feared Keith might never settle down.

As much as Keith had wanted Jay to be there, he had anticipated his absence. Over the years, he'd grown accustomed to Jay's disappearances, particularly on dates that were important to Keith. It was as if he disliked events and rituals that he saw as trivial.

Nonetheless, Keith had to admit his friend had always been there for Abby. Ever since her birth, he'd been present at her birthday parties and graduations and had even paid for her wedding. Keith had wanted to pay for it, but Jay had written a check on the spot that had allowed Abby and Tom to plan a true fairytale wedding.

Keith sometimes quietly sensed that, to Sam, her first wedding with more than seven hundred guests would always be her *real* wedding.

Indeed, to Sam, her second wedding had been a fun little evening of heavy heat and heavier drinking. They didn't even take a honeymoon because they were going to take a trip later that year with the girls.

Their wedding night, the newlyweds simply took the drive back home to the girls and a sleepy babysitter who had driven them home earlier in the evening.

When they woke up the next morning, the girls were there, as they always were, rushing to their bed as soon as they heard their mom and Keith awake. Emma exuded natural excitement and Andrea reserved curiosity. Keith could sense that on this day of great importance to him, the girls saw mostly the irrefutable fact that their parents would never be together again.

At the same time, the foundation of their marriage was set in stone as the new family slowly moved in the soft flow of simplicity and beauty.

This was the first time Keith had ever lived with children, and he loved hearing Andrea and Emma playing upstairs.

A certain day during those first few months in Dallas stood out as significant. Andrea's teacher had invited parents to visit the class, and each child had memorized a brief poem to recite. Andrea was just nine, and Keith had seen her practicing for days.

When Sam and Keith arrived, Sam immediately walked around greeting children and parents with ease and friendliness. Even in such a short span of time, she knew everybody. As Keith took a seat toward the back of the class, a girl with big eyes and pigtails came up to him.

"You're Andrea's dad, aren't you?" she asked.

"Well, not exactly. I'm married to her mom, which..."

The young girl interrupted, "Yeah, I know all about that. I'm ten you know." She ruined her initial impression of sophistication by saying, "So, you're her uncle now, right?"

"I'm her stepdad. You know what that means? By the way, what's your name?"

"Elisa. What's yours?"

"I'm Keith."

"So you're her stepdad. Cool." She paused for a moment and said, "What's a stepdad exactly?"

"I'm married to Andrea's mom, but Andrea has her own dad."

"Oh, now I get it. Is he here?"

"No, he couldn't make it."

"Yeah, my dad couldn't come, either," she said, looking around the room, perhaps hoping her father would show up after all.

Andrea walked past, and Keith said, "Are you ready, Andy?"

"Sure," she replied, all but pretending she didn't know him.

Keith didn't take it personally since he realized she had reached that age when parents become more a source of embarrassment than pride and affection.

As the two girls moved toward the front of the class and people settled in their seats, Keith overheard their words.

"Your dad came to see you. Mine didn't," Elisa said with a bit of admiration.

"He's my *stepdad*, not my real dad."

"But he came, and that's what counts."

Although Sam, Andrea, Emma, and Keith came together as a family, Keith and Emma were inseparable from the start.

There were times when Emma wanted Keith to tuck her in bed or help her with her homework. She would sit on his lap and snuggle beside him as they watched TV with an ease that came naturally to both, so much so that Keith occasionally wondered if Sam felt a bit left out.

One night, Keith walked into Emma's room to tuck her in. As he turned the light out and was about to leave, the sleepy little girl said, "Nightie night, Daddy."

Keith froze in surprise and a touch of pride, knowing some clarification or correction needed to be made. She was too quick, though.

"I called you *Daddy*," she said with a slight giggle.

"Well, that's okay. It sounds nice, but you already have a daddy, you know."

"Of course, silly. But maybe I should have two daddies. Besides, you are like a daddy. You know how I know?" she teased, wanting him to join in the game.

"Because I take you to school in the morning?"

"No."

"Because I go to your soccer games with your mommy?"

Still an emphatic "No" came from the darkness.

"Because I fixed your bike the first time we met? Or tried to fix it at least?"

"Uh uh."

"Well, it's getting late and you should probably tell me."

"Because you kissed my owie on the knee the other day and made it better. That's how! And only mommies and daddies can do that. Everybody knows that!"

"Good night, Emma."

"Good night...*Keith*," she giggled.

As he closed the door, he promised himself he'd remember this night for a lifetime.

"Your daughter just called me daddy. It was half accident and half confusion and half plain teasing," he told Sam as he got into bed a few minutes later.

"That's too many halves, but who's counting? I'm guessing Emma?"

"Who else?"

"Andrea, of course."

"No, she's pretty clear on who's who."

"They both adore you, you know."

"I do. And I adore them, too."

"I know you do. That's exactly why I love you."

"And I thought it was my classic good looks and irresistible charisma."

"Well, that, too!"

"And what about this surprise I have for you under the covers. Does that make you love me?"

"Pervert!"

A while later, out of the blue, Sam asked, "Honey, are you sure you'll be okay without us having a baby of our own?"

"We made a deal, Sam. It would mean starting out for me, and for you it would be going back to a past you've left behind. Imagine us with a baby. We'd need diapers, a crib, bottles, strollers, all that stuff. Where would we put it?"

"Keith, look at me. This is important. Are you okay with us not having kids?"

He thought for a moment before answering. "A big part of me says yes, Sam. Will there always be a little bit of doubt? Probably, yes. But we've come a long way in a short time. And I really think we're fine. I want you happy, and I want the girls happy."

"Sometimes I've wondered what it would have been like to have met earlier in life," Sam mused. "For you to be my children's father."

"We are who we are, and I'm sure there's a reason why things happened the way they have."

"As long as you're okay, I don't see myself going through all that again. But I also don't want you having regrets about it later on."

"We're fine, sweetie. We really are."

Before sleep took them, Sam called him in the voice he was so used to by now.

"Come here, my love," she whispered, opening her arms, her body, and her heart for him to fill.

He went to her with the hunger and urgency that many years later he'd attempt to remember before the terrible words passed between them. That urgency had been inaugurated on a windy evening long ago when their bodies gave in to the inevitable collision they both so desired.

———————◆◆◆◆◆◆◆◆◆◆———————

These were Keith's thoughts as he continued meandering through the old city center.

It was a different city now. Some of the landmarks of his youth were gone: the restaurant where he had occasionally sat with his father for a late Sunday breakfast, the small movie house where he'd gone on his first date as a teenager, the sports apparel store in one of the tiny commercial passages that crisscrossed some of the buildings where his parents had taken him to buy the countless pairs of tennis shoes he'd gone through as a kid. Those places were gone.

Then the cathedral bells rang. Keith realized that, in a few hours, Jay would arrive. He realized he wasn't even sure where Jay was coming from. It was part of the mystery always emanating from his friend. What would it be like to see him? What would they talk about?

Keith wasn't sure of the answer.

Chapter 7

Following the sound of the church bells, Keith slowly walked away from the heart of the downtown area. Moving west, he soon reached the patios surrounding the cathedral.

Without any defined purpose, he guided his rambling thoughts to the beginning of his relationship with Samantha, specifically to the physical nature of their love. She had an animal instinct that had caught him by surprise all those years ago when desire finally won its freedom.

They'd had dinner in Mexico City one afternoon, and the evening had progressed like the many preceding it. Long conversations had allowed them to get to know each other better and deeper while drinks had lubricated their thoughts and touches. They'd held hands and felt ever closer, but, in the end, Samantha had to leave to pick up her kids.

Another afternoon a short while later had been different. Keith remembered delicious slivers of that day.

"I don't have to pick up the girls until late tonight."

Nothing more was said as they drove to Keith's apartment. Nothing more needed to be said. Their eyes spoke for them.

Keith opened the door, and Sam lunged into his arms. They had both waited a long time for this encounter of physical certainty they both desperately needed. It was one of those amazing moments when hearts, bodies, and souls find shared and perfect alignment.

Eagerness and anticipation converged. As their need for each other overtook them, their shared solitude shed its skin and allowed them to truly see each other in the pale light.

The apartment shadows grew longer and darker. The door to the terrace stood open, and the cool wind swept through, the long curtains billowing as if dancing to the music of the spheres.

As the afternoon faded into dusk and then night, the ritual of bodies dancing took place. Sam's impatience was strong as Keith's longing broke.

That day, the boy and the girl of yesterday became strong warriors in the ancestral combat of striking kisses and furious caresses. Their souls gave in to the rhythms that their bodies now dictated. As their legs and breathing tangled, they found long-lost territory that had the feel of the familiar and memories of a previous existence even as it was new and worth exploring with attention. More than a discovery, it felt like a long-awaited return to a place they had visited eons before.

They examined each other with the hunger of scavengers and the attention of archeologists. They probed and tasted and gave of each other, biting with care.

She offered him her soft lips and open legs. She gave him warm whispers that urged him on with words that rose to unspeakable cries. He covered her mouth with kisses, with warmth and words of his own that went from tribute to anguished answers to her cries.

In time, they found a common cadence, a rhythm that answered their unspoken questions and, of course, a question that would always need an answer. They moved and were moved by each other and by the beating of each other's hearts, keeping time.

As their love reignited, it was an explosive mixture of sounds, movements, and scents that came and went back in time to queens and round tables. Swords were struck, and gaping wounds gushed the blood of warriors, alarmed by the proximity of an end. But inside the castle, their battle, an even more ancestral one, resumed.

They screamed in both their native and adopted tongues. The Spanish words insisted on monosyllables.

"*Sí.*"

"*Más.*"

"*Más.*"

"*Más!*"

"*Así.*"

Words grew and became louder.

"*Bésame.*"

"*Cógeme.*"

"*Dame duro.*"

"*Así!*"

The words in English became beautifully loud and vulgar.

"I love you in me."

"There. There."

"Again."

"Let me kiss you, lick you."

"More."

"Fuck me."

"Harder."

"Harder!"

"Oh, God!"

The prayer was a steady crescendo.

Fortissimo.

They moaned and screamed in this mixed chant now used to incite, to subjugate, to conquer as swords plunged deep and daggers pierced skin.

It was the most fundamental convergence of man and woman, and in it, they found a joy and passion each had suspected. Once the aftershocks subsided, they lay tangled in each other, waiting, knowing that in this moment, in these very arms, life was meant to be lived.

Awaking from the spell, they looked at each other, seeking a simple sign to confirm that this wasn't a dream. That it was her body and her pale nakedness that had indeed collided with his body and his nakedness, a shade less pale but amazed and grateful nonetheless.

The peace of their stillness weaved itself into a glow. It was then that Sam decided she would follow Keith and accept his wish to join their lives to become something as close to a family as they could possibly create.

As Samantha pondered a *forever* that, unbeknownst to her, would always elude her, sleep overcame them both.

Later that evening, Sam woke up and saw Keith naked and fast asleep. She snuggled close to his body, taking in his warmth, his smell, and his peaceful, rhythmic breathing.

She drove home that night smiling, with a slight and pleasant throbbing between her legs.

Once home, she checked on the girls. Although they each had their own room, it was inevitable that Emma would go into her older sister's room to cuddle, and so they were that night.

Andrea lay stretched on her side, her beautiful profile and dark hair spread like a spider web on the pillow. Emma, entwined in her sister's embrace, with her mouth slightly open in the faintest of smiles, looked as though she were dreaming the sweetest of dreams.

After they married, it was Keith who would walk into Emma's room only to find the tiny bed empty and rumpled. He would then find her in Andrea's room, one door down, bunched into a small ball of warmth in the arms of her older sister, her perpetual guardian.

For a short time, Keith wondered if they should each stay in their own room, but the girls' need for each other would accept no rules. It was too strong and had been there since the beginning of time, their time, as well as the time of other sisters before them.

On this first day of physically consummating their union, lying in his own bed after Sam slipped away, Keith could not believe the amazing woman he had held just a few hours before.

He could still sense her presence. There was the warmth and dampness she'd left on the bed as silent testimony. There was her glass of water resting on the night table. There was an ashtray with a few barely smoked cigarettes. There was her perfume, subtly moving about the room.

The curtains billowed as he crossed the hallway to close the windows.

He walked into the bathroom and saw the rumpled towels and a pair of her earrings by the sink, so lonely, so utterly feminine, so seemingly out of place.

As he had years earlier, but now a bit more knowingly, Keith mentally clicked away, forever storing these simple images, magnifying their meaning, taking permanent inventory of Sam's presence, bathing these images in the light of certainty.

He felt an immediacy that captured the present without truly anticipating its implications in an imperfect future. Not because he was incapable of understanding the syllogisms derived from his emotions but because an imperfect future simply didn't exist.

Little did he know that he would look for these and other signs of Sam's presence for years after she had left with the same urgency and conviction with which she'd taken his hand and led him to bed. The night after they had first shared a bed, Keith began writing a small poem for Sam. He never finished it until years later and titled it *The Kiss of That Boy and That Girl*. It was a simple tribute that had crossed his mind and he had decided to write it down. As their relationship changed, so did the words until one day he thought it was finished. For years after, he had regretted not keeping a copy, although some of the lines were embedded in his mind and in his heart forever.

These brief memories, these immutable images, lingered, remained hidden in the shadows, refusing to leave his mind years later as he revisited his life, now at another stage, walking the dusty streets of Cuernavaca, waiting for Jay.

But on that evening, not quite lost in the memory of a seventy-four-year-old man, the only thing that truly mattered was the simple fact that, at that very instant, and without truly knowing it yet, Keith had begun to need Sam.

Chapter 8

As much as the streets of Cuernavaca represented the distant past, they also meant the more immediate past that Keith shared with his daughter. He and Sam had taken Abby to Cuernavaca for the first time when she was a few months old, and they'd returned periodically as Abby grew up.

Although both Sam and Keith had wonderful memories of their childhoods in Cuernavaca, their lives were now elsewhere. It was Sam who remained more connected to her adoptive hometown through friends and the fact that the girls' father still lived there.

In spite of inheriting his parents' home, Keith was less interested in visiting. In part, this was because his friends had moved away years before but also because he saw the beauty of the city of his childhood inexorably eroding with each passing visit.

And so it was that Abby came to Cuernavaca from time to time. As she grew a little older, she became eager to learn where her parents had lived, where they had gone to school, and where they had met.

Abby, the little girl who remained Keith's true north for a lifetime.

The year Abby was born was one of the happiest periods in Keith's life. The anticipation was amazing for the entire family.

As far as Keith was concerned, Abby was a chance of renewal for Sam, a time to feel as she had when her other two daughters were born and she herself was younger if a bit overwhelmed by the vicissitudes of life.

Keith was admittedly bewildered by Sam's initial reaction when she found out she was pregnant. Rather than the typical exhilaration most expectant moms experience, Sam had cried for a full day.

He had kiddingly asked if she might be pregnant after a particularly crabby week. Sam had immediately said no, but Keith had walked to the supermarket and purchased a pregnancy test that had promptly turned blue.

Still unconvinced, Sam had refused to admit she was pregnant to Keith or to herself, so Keith went out and bought another pregnancy test, which also turned blue. As they both realized that Sam was irrefutably pregnant, she began to cry.

Keith had walked into the bathroom in time to see her grab the pregnancy tests and their wrappers and throw them furiously into the small trash container under the sink. Staring at the mirror, she'd begun to cry, softly murmuring, "No, no, no. This can't be happening."

Keith had never understood Sam's reaction and had always attributed it to some womanly moment of temporary insanity.

To Keith, knowing he'd finally be a father was a turning point. He and Sam had been married for two years now, and he was scared and delighted all at the same time. He loved Sam for this sign of their love, even though the pregnancy had been a surprise, even though they'd agreed not to have a child. Although both were nearing forty, he believed this unexpected baby, this gift, would give them renewed youth and strength.

Eventually Samantha overcame her initial shock and joined in the delight of Jay and Emma and Andrea, who were thrilled by the idea of a baby sister. It was a time of wonderful contentment for the family. It seemed that happiness grew even as Sam's belly did, and Keith came to realize that Sam was born to be a mother. She emanated an understanding of the world and of her children that seemed to come from somewhere below the Earth. It was a connection to life in the most fundamental of ways.

The months flew by, and soon the entire family was overcome by the festiveness of Christmas and the excitement of a newborn expected to arrive the first week in January.

Keith could always count on his good friend Jay to bring a down-to-earth irreverence to any situation. Jay had come to visit a few weeks before Christmas, bringing gifts for the girls and for the yet-to-be-born child. As always, his gifts were extravagant: matching gold bracelets from Van Cleef for Andrea and Emma and a number of tiny little designer outfits for the baby. Jay's generosity toward the girls never ended. Well into their becoming young independent women, he'd always been there with gifts that seemed outlandish. Never from a sense of extravagance, but rather from a lack of abidance to social convention. That was Jay. He never set out to break the rules. It was more like he simply was unaware they existed. Particularly toward Abby he had always shown a generosity beyond belief. From birthdays to the day of her wedding, he inundated her with presents. Through the years, Keith wondered if that affection was a way for Jay to compensate for his absence in his own daughter's life.

As their conversation moved from topic to topic one predictably tequila-soaked night, Jay bluntly aimed to put things in perspective, or at least in his perspective, namely raunchy, sometimes almost disgusting, yet invariably good-humored.

"So, Sam is having a kid, eh?" he laughed.

"Pretty amazing, right?"

"Better make sure the little fucker is yours. You know how women are. They're all sluts, and they all have a price."

"They are not all sluts, Jay. You know that somewhere in that hard head of yours."

"Dream on, Miller. Always on the side of women. Just wait until you get fucked the way I have."

"Well, for some reason I think Sam is the good kind of woman. But, then again, you never know."

"Dude, women cheat as much as we do. You're the one with the big, hard head, and you definitely don't get women. Who do you think married men cheat with? Inflatable dolls? No! Married women, of course. I sometimes tried to be faithful. Then one day I said, 'Fuck it. *No es lo mío la monogamia.*' Monogamy is not for me. Not then, not now. Cheating in a relationship is a way of bringing balance. You cheat, she cheats, and everyone is happy. Don't tell me you've never cheated on Sam? With all the traveling you do, you've never had *un buen palo*, a great lay, my dear Miller?"

Keith laughed as he always did, both at the strange accent that Jay had developed having grown up in Cuernavaca and Madrid as well as at his expression, so Spaniard at times, so Mexican the next moment. At times, there was even a little Texan thrown into the mix.

"Jay, some people do; some people don't." Keith wasn't the slightest bit tempted to bite.

"C'mon, Keith. What the fuck is that supposed to mean? Have you ever fucked a woman other than Sam since you got married? It's a *yes* or *no* answer."

"Truth is, I haven't."

"Mother fucker! What about that fox that worked with you? The girl from Spain, what was her name? Nelly, Naty? Nuria! That's the one. She looked like she'd fuck your eyeballs out. She probably liked it in the ass."

"You fucking pig." Keith laughed at the lewd, raunchy humor of his friend.

"What? Like it never crossed your mind? When did you become such a hypocrite, Miller?"

"It crossed my mind," Keith admitted.

"So you did fuck her," Jay insisted.

"Actually, I didn't."

"What about that girl in Austin? You know, someone's niece?"

"Jay, I tried. I swear to God I wanted to fuck Melissa. I called her, but I backed out once we were in the room."

"You are such a *pussy*! What the fuck is wrong with you?"

"Nothing. The fact is, Sam means everything to me. I don't want to fuck it up."

"We'll see how that works out for you."

<hr />

Melissa was the only time Keith had been really tempted and came damn close to cheating on Sam.

The niece of a friend, she was ten years younger than Sam, dark haired, with alabaster skin. And she was very much married.

Much to Keith's surprise, they had been instantly attracted to each other.

On his way home from dropping Andrea and Emma at summer camp, he'd stopped in Austin to spend the night after a long day of driving. Yes, he'd timed it almost intentionally so that he'd arrive in the late afternoon. He'd called Sam and told her he'd be home the next day.

As soon as he hung up with Sam, he'd called Melissa. He felt guilty, but his urge pushed him on. She had a dark, brooding look. She was different. She was not Sam.

Many thoughts crossed his mind as he made that call. There was shame, fear, and excitement, oddly combined, forming a knot in his stomach. He'd heard from Jay how simple, how ordinary, such a decision was. Years later, he'd look back and think that maybe his love for Sam had somehow faded, that the everyday bickering had triggered the urge to betray, to break vows. But that day, it was simple unadulterated lust that allowed him to dial those numbers.

"Hello, this is Melissa," he heard. "Can't take your call, but leave me a message, and I'll get back to you."

Keith did not leave a message, but he knew, or at least hoped, she'd recognize his number.

He drove downtown and found the hotel owned by his friend Scotty, an old cowboy with a leather face and whisky-seared voice who was perpetually stoned on some of the Southwest's best weed.

Scott was there, as always, behind the front desk with a glass in his hand and a smile on his face, both signs of a life lived well.

"Well, well, if it isn't Mr. Miller himself." The hotelier stood up and came from behind the counter, his smile opening wider as he embraced his friend.

"Shit, Scotty. You must have a pact with Dorian Gray. You don't look a day older than seventy," Keith teased.

"And fuck you, too, Buddy. Seventy, eighty, take your pick. All I know is that I can still kick your cracker ass."

"I would never hit an old fucker like you. I have too much respect for my elders. My momma taught me well."

"Well, out of respect, I won't tell you what your momma taught *me*."

"That's cold, you son of a bitch. But it's still good to see you."

"And what on earth brings you to my humble abode? You need a room? Got the family with you?"

"No, Scotty. It's just my lonesome self, visiting an old friend. And I do need a room. As to what brings me to your fine establishment, well, I hear women like to fuck in these finely appointed rooms of yours. Thought I'd see if the legend is true."

"Oh, so now the truth spills out. And to answer your question, Keith, it must be true 'cause people keep coming back. And there is some major fucking going on. At least that's what the girls who clean the rooms tell me. I hear some incredible stories of rodents, donkeys, and midgets."

"So business is going well? I've seen a couple of articles. One in *Texas Monthly*. You're getting great reviews."

"I raise the prices and people still come back. I'm booked solid for the next six months. Can you believe it? This place is making more money than I could ever need. One thing I never thought I'd be was rich. Here I am, sitting on my ass all day, smoking weed and drinking wine, making millions! There sure is a fucking God above looking out for us good people!"

They laughed as Scotty poured Keith a welcome drink straight from under the counter.

"*Salud!*" they toasted in unison.

"I think if there is a God, Scotty, he's just fucking with my head," Keith confessed, only half in jest. "I have an MBA, work my ass off, and don't know if I'll be able to pay for the girls to go to college. You have a guitar, a bong, and you're making millions. Shit!"

"That's 'cause you worry too much, my dear friend. You simply worry too fucking much. You always have... "

After a few minutes of friendly conversation, with a second glass of the smoothest, smokiest tequila Keith had tasted in months, he walked to his room, an amazing suite that Scott had refused to let him pay for.

As he opened the door, his phone rang, and he recognized the area code instantly. "Hi, Melissa," he answered with a smile and a bit of nervousness.

"You called? What a surprise, Keith. It's not my birthday. It's not Christmas. So I thought to myself, why would my old friend Keith suddenly call? And so, intrigued, I'm calling back."

"Want to grab a drink?" he asked, not wasting time.

"What, no 'How have you been? How are things going? How are your children?' Just like that?"

"Is that a maybe?" he teased.

She laughed. "It could be a maybe. Don't tell me you're in Austin."

"I am. I'm near downtown Austin at my friend Scott's hotel. And it happens to have a great little courtyard where some of the best margaritas in the world are made."

"Keith, are you sure?"

"Sure of what, Melissa? I'm calling my old friend to see if she wants to have a drink. Must you make it so damn hard?"

"Well..."

"It's sounding like a maybe. The hotel is the Hacienda Francesca, I think the address is..." He fumbled with notes on the night table looking for anything that might have the hotel's address, but she interrupted him.

"I know where it is. I'll be there in twenty."

A short while later, they sat on the patio, speaking softly. After the fourth margarita, she asked if the rooms were nice, and he felt something stir in his groin.

"Have you never stayed here?"

"No, never have."

Keith thought about what might happen and forged on. "Want to come up and see for yourself?"

She didn't answer but took her glass and her purse as she stood up, saying so much without a single word being spoken.

They stumbled into his room, drinks in hand. Soon, mouth on mouth and body against body, the breathing became heavier and clothes flew. Even though Keith wanted this, had planned this, as they fumbled in the darkness with buckles and straps, he was suddenly overcome with guilt, with thoughts of Sam, and told her, "I can't do this."

"Here, let me get it," she said, doing that tricky, inexplicable move with which women undo their bras that men never learned and probably never will.

"No, Mel. I can't do this."

"What? Let me help you."

"No, stop. This, Mel. I can't...be here with you. I shouldn't be here with you. I'm married, you're married, and you're my friend. And I want to be able to always look you in the eye." Not to mention look Sam in the eye. "I'm sorry."

"You know what, Keith?" she said as she turned the lamp on and began to gather her clothes. "I should be all teary-eyed, thinking what a gentleman you are and how your wife should be all proud and shit. And I should agree that we are friends."

She paused. He saw the anger in her eyes and thought for a moment she was going to reach out and slap him. He backed away.

"But right now, the truth is that I'm pretty pissed. In fact, I'm very fucking pissed. I just don't get your sick little game."

She stood up. "Don't call again," she hissed as she picked up her shoes. A second before the door closed, she pushed it back open and said, "Fuck you, Keith Miller."

As she walked out, she loudly slammed the door.

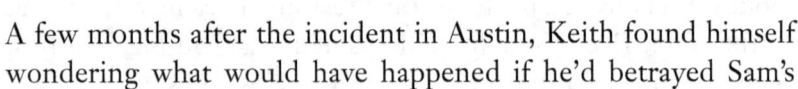

A few months after the incident in Austin, Keith found himself wondering what would have happened if he'd betrayed Sam's trust, his marriage, the girls.

He then surprised himself by asking whether things were okay in his marriage. Until now, he'd given it little conscious thought. They were settling into their fifth year as a family, and Abby was going on three. With her arrival, he'd assumed nothing would ever alter the course of their relationship, but lately something had seemed wrong.

Maybe it was his own doubts surfacing as he tried to forgive himself for seeking his friend Melissa in Austin. The guilt had been nagging him. He had wondered if perhaps telling Sam about the incident would be a way of showing his shame and at the same time his commitment to their relationship. And he naturally asked himself what Sam would do, or maybe even had done, in such a situation, such a moment of truth. But, as is often the case, neither one of them knew what the future had in store for them.

He recalled an incident of unexpected sharpness. To Samantha, appearances were of paramount importance. He just didn't realize how much they mattered until one day she made fun of his appearance and growing hair loss. She did it with a smile, but Keith learned then and there that Samantha was capable of a shallowness he'd never suspected.

The incident occurred on their way to a friend's funeral. Not a very close friend but a good neighbor who had fallen victim to a brutal, relentless cancer that had consumed him in months.

As they were about to get in the car, Sam had asked, "Why are you wearing that tie? It doesn't look good."

"Sam, we're going to a funeral, not a party. Let's just go."

"Well, if you want to look like that, it's your problem, but since your appearance reflects on me, it's kind of my problem, too."

"What's the matter with you? This is a fine and expensive suit. I've worn it with this tie and shirt a thousand times. You've never said anything before."

"That's the problem, Keith. You *have* worn it a thousand times. It's time to change things up a bit. And what's with the hair? Could it be that style is supposed to cover the fact that you're losing it?" She smiled, but her eyes were sharp and unfriendly.

"Not at all. I just haven't combed it like this in a while. What's up with you?"

"You just don't look good."

"We're driving to say farewell to a friend we both loved. Let's not fight, Sam. Not now. Please."

They drove in silence, but that night in bed, Keith brought up the afternoon's conversation.

"Hey, I'm sure it's Rick's funeral that got us down this afternoon. Why would God choose him? Imagine how hard it will be on Adrienne and the kids. We should spend time with them, have them over for dinner. Things like that."

"Yeah, I guess," Samantha said without much conviction.

"She's been a good friend. She suffered a hell of a lot through Rick's illness and now she's all alone. The hardest part is still ahead. The fact that she's alone with the kids will gradually sink in."

"I'm sure she'd love to hear those words of encouragement."

"They're true. She'll need you, is all I'm saying."

"I know that, Keith, for the love of Christ!"

Anger appeared without provocation, and Keith sighed, not wanting to get into an argument.

"We are lucky and blessed, Sam. We have each other and the girls, a great home, we do things we enjoy."

"I'm not sure we're all that lucky."

"Why would you say that?"

"I don't know, Keith. Sometimes I feel like life is passing us by. Work. Run. The kids. More work. There's gotta be more. Doesn't there, Keith? Please tell me there's more."

"Well, for what it's worth, you have a guy who's crazy about you."

"I don't doubt it," she mumbled, turning away and reaching to turn off the light.

Lying in bed next to her silent husband, Sam knew she had hurt him. She knew criticizing him would hurt his masculinity, yet she'd done it anyway, and she didn't care how he felt.

On his side of the bed, Keith lay stricken, both by the realization that Sam wasn't exactly the woman he'd thought she was and by the fact that he was starting to see her differently. He'd always felt she possessed a sensitivity that came from the Earth and from the millions of years of womanhood she embodied, but now his dream was beginning to crack.

He was beginning to realize she was somewhat shallow and bitter, and he didn't understand why. He wondered if this might be why he'd been so drawn to Melissa. Yet in spite of it all, including his momentary urge to stray, he never doubted his love for Sam. It was there. Constant. Simple. True.

Nonetheless, day after day, a dark shadow began to slowly and cruelly grow, blocking out their love. They held hands less frequently. They spoke the words of daily life, but there was an undercurrent disconnecting them that even Andrea and Emma began to notice.

Keith woke up one morning stricken with the knowledge that something was very wrong in his marriage. He couldn't trace the events that led to its unraveling. For years, he'd felt that he and Sam had somehow managed to remain a part of each other's dreams. Every night, as sleep won over the anxieties and events of the day, he'd felt they shared a territory of far away but interwoven thoughts.

But then one night, he realized their dreams were their own. Each was dreaming in another dimension. His dreams were about his incessant fear of losing her and of building bridges that would connect their lives. He sensed that Sam's were about her desperate need to get away from God knows what.

Increasingly, he felt that what she wanted to get away from was him.

Chapter 9

U nable to comprehend what was happening, equally unable to reach Sam in conversation, Keith did the only thing he could think of to do: he wrote to her.

Though he didn't know her plans, he knew in his heart that their relationship was fraying. He wrote to Sam in a last desperate attempt to salvage it.

How do we convince ourselves that,
inevitably,
the seeming ease of ordinary and shared life
puts in constant state of siege the small isle
on which we buried
the treasures of tenderness
since we set out on this tandem travel?

And we buried these treasures precisely to consecrate them,
to know forever where to find them.

But we forgot, innocently, to leave a trace, an unequivocal print,
or at least a hint as to where to find them anew.

It seems to be the inexorable path of love,
but let us throw a lifesaver at this love.
Not love in the abstract, the generality of love,
not to the love of the movies we love,
especially if based on true stories.
No, not at that love,
not because that one doesn't move us,
but because that one is not enough.

Let us save our love.
Let us give it wings,
let us propel it,
let us give it reasons.

Even if I don't attempt to dictate it,
but barely propose it,
let's invent for it a new insanity,
a different look,
and allow yourself the gift of a surprise from me.

Let us take love out into the sunshine
so that it can get some freckles and contrasts.
We will cover it with fragrant oils and with our hearts
as it peels and leaves a newer, shinier love.

Let us find the treasures, our tenderness,
and the dreams we once founded.
And then, definitively, let us unbury them.
For the love of love,
buried they serve us no purpose.
Let us place them on the highest prairies
even if dust lessens their brightness.

We will polish these dreams with kisses and hands held.
Then let us take them all to the purest beach we know so well,

there where we know the tides and the coves.
And on that day, the sun and our children,
as old friends,
will play with costumes
of warmth and deep brown skins.

Let us undo love with rigor,
so when we make love, it will be again with our souls,
bare as our bodies.

Let us forget people and money for a while,
not because we don't care
or have forgotten them
but because they aren't enough to save our love.

It seems to be the inexorable path of love
that laziness will overcome not only our bones
but our ever-tired joy
whose silent and deadly scream is not heard evermore.

It is the day when words and eyes become knives and treason.
And that day, with a vengeance, let us save our love.
Let us praise it and weep humbly before its inevitable victory.

Through the cities we wander, along with our melancholy,
let us have love walk with us.
After all, love and melancholy sometimes sound so like one another
that nobody is alarmed at this confusion.

Let us save our love
at every turn,
every encounter,
every duel
so that man and woman see each other from within.

Let us water the dry parched earth where our bitter words have fallen.
Only then will they lose themselves amongst the shit and the mud,
which we will naturally not step on ever again.

Let us save our love, the one today, the one tomorrow,
the one that's written with a capital L.
Let us save our love that pleads for forgiveness for having been distracted.
Let us keep our love always warm, like the funeral pyre for a dead daughter,
like the promise forever kept close.
Let us save our love.

As Keith tried to remember some of the lines of the poem all those years later, he realized how futile the attempt had been. It was as if he'd tried to write to a woman who cared about the written word, a woman who could be touched and moved by the beauty of language. Of course, at the time, he'd had no idea that Sam wasn't that woman.

As he reminisced, Keith thought how that poem, those lines, had probably never even been read, much less resonated or made sense to the woman he loved.

Chapter 10

I t was sunny the day Keith strolled into the house at Rose's ranch to pick up Abby and learned that his wife was having an affair.

Rose had the good sense to leave Abby in the adjoining living room while she guided Keith to the kitchen. His first thought was that she was going to ask him to stay for lunch, but instead, she said she had news he ought to hear.

"Keith, Sam is seeing someone, and has been for some time."

At first Keith thought he'd heard something else. He stopped and looked at her. "What are you telling me, Rose?"

"The truth. You deserve the truth, and it seems nobody has the guts to let you in on it. Even some of the people you count on as friends. She's involved with someone, Keith. They're making plans: living arrangements, whatnot. Sam is going to ask you for a divorce. She's already spoken to a lawyer. You don't have to believe me, but I know where she is right now. She's with him, if you want to go confront them."

He never did. It wasn't the way he handled things. He felt there needed to be a level of maturity and integrity that the obvious confrontation would shatter. He found out later who Sam was seeing and for how long it had been going on when the photos and letters began trickling in.

The letters came one by one, anonymous notes detailing the dates and places of Sam's encounters with her lover. He was baffled by the letters, by the obvious poison in them clearly meant to humiliate him even beyond the brutal truth itself.

He showed them to Sam wishing she'd explain them, dismiss them as blatant, hurtful lies, but she said nothing. Her silence was her admission. Later, as the relationship faded and the words became cold, brutal, and bitter, Sam accused him, saying Keith himself had written the letters.

Yet it was obvious that only Sam, or someone close to her, could have known the details they contained. More hurtful than anything else was the revelation that she sometimes took the girls with her under the guise of friendly group gatherings.

Then one afternoon Keith saw her camera, and the photos it contained revealed the extent of her betrayal. There were photos of Sam and her lover in their own home, in their own bedroom, that revealed more than letters themselves ever could. It seemed to Keith that Sam had intentionally sent the letters and left the camera where he could find it to avoid the simple, honest explanation that Keith thought he deserved but that she would never grant. Simple words that could have meant a decent closure to their story.

As the vicious truths came forth, so did an endless cascade of betrayals and lies that entered Keith's heart like knives. If only Sam had been honest enough to tell him, it could have been less devastating. Sure, he would have hurt, but her utter lack of integrity was unfathomable.

But that came later. Now, as Rose continued speaking, Keith momentarily lost his balance. There was no discernible tone in her voice. She stated the facts flatly, almost brutally. Keith knew that behind the harsh words, she cared; that was obvious from the brightness of her eyes, but he stopped listening. He wanted to run away. Run to Sam, but, after all, that was now pointless.

In the back of his mind, Keith wondered if Rose was secretly happy that this was happening. Perhaps this was her moment of triumph. Rose and Sam had always fought, so perhaps this was irresistible ammunition. Then again, for some reason, Rose didn't necessarily seem to like Keith. Keith never really knew why, since he had always been nice to Sam's family. Sure, they'd had trivial disagreements, but nothing more.

Keith was quite liberal in the eyes of many, especially where it concerned Sam's two daughters. He encouraged them to read books that other parents considered inappropriate. He talked candidly about drugs, sex, and the hazards and wonders of growing up. He even served the girls wine for dinner.

He had been raised that way and thought of himself as well adjusted, educated, and successful. As far as he was concerned, there was nothing wrong with the way he helped Sam raise the girls, whom he sincerely adored.

Then again, most people never realized that the girls weren't his real daughters. The only thing a keen observer would notice was that the two older girls called him "Keith" or "K," never "Dad" or "Daddy" as most girls called their fathers at that age.

Keith suspected that Rose in particular believed that while Sam was too tolerant in some areas and in general too selfish, Keith himself was too extreme, either excessively permissive or overly strict and harsh with the girls.

You never knew with Rose. Keith was always caught between her uncanny charm and her momentary outbursts of anger. Maybe it was simply that she was a woman. Keith had always struggled to understand the opposite sex, from his mother to his wife to his daughters to the other women who had played a role in his life.

"I told you years ago, Keith. Be careful with my sister. She walked out on her first marriage, and she'll do it again. She's always been so selfish! I am so mad at her right now!"

"We'll see, Rose."

"Believe me, Keith. There is no *we'll see*. Sam is three steps ahead of you. And watch who you talk to. Get a lawyer and take good care of those kids. And I mean all three girls, not just Abigail."

Rose was the only person, along with her grandmother Nelly when she was still alive, who called Abby by her given name.

"There's only Abby, Rose. Emma and Andrea are not my children." Even as he spoke the words in hurt and anger, Keith knew they weren't entirely true.

"They aren't, Keith? Really? Do you really believe that?"

As Keith and Rose walked silently to his car for the warm drive north to Dallas, she asked that in return for telling him the truth that he promise to never tell Sam that she was the one who had told him about the affair. He kept this promise all his life. He always felt it was a way of proving to Sam's family that he was a man whose word meant something. He knew they didn't care, but he did, and he knew that Abby would too, someday.

"I'm sorry Keith. I really am. I hoped it would end differently for you and my sister. She just doesn't learn. Poor, immature woman. But...she's my sister, Keith."

In the end, as the years passed, he felt grateful to Rose for her brutal honesty, and they cultivated a respectful friendship that endured for years, even after her own husband and sister both passed away. It helped that Abby loved her Aunt Rose. Keith always made sure he kept his daughter as close as possible to her aunt. Keith saw in Rose's brown eyes the eyes of his own daughter, passed from generation to generation.

But now, having learned the wrenching truth, he buckled Abby into her car seat, his mind racing, inventing stories and images that cut deep. After leaving the gates of Rose's property, he pulled over, retched on the grassy side of the country lane, and began to cry silently. After a few minutes, he looked into the backseat. His daughter was peering out the window, too young to comprehend that something of enormous consequence had just happened.

Keith composed himself with an effort when the little girl smiled at him with the toothy grin she had inherited from him and that invariably melted his heart. Abby was to become a source of precarious balance in his life. Throughout his life, she was always his compass, his true north.

But there was a time when everything was different.

After Abby was born, Keith and Abby were inseparable. As she grew, at night, she and Keith would play little games with words, questions, and answers that he believed would help his daughter learn to love words as much as he did.

"Who's my true north?" he asked Abby every night at bedtime.

"I am," she always replied with a smile, loving this little ritual without understanding what her father meant. This was one of several rituals they played that helped define their sense of belonging to each other. Some came and went while others were kept for a lifetime.

"And why are you my true north?"

"Because I point you in the right direction," she would say in her tiny voice, pointing a finger.

"You sure do, kiddo. Time to turn off the lights. Good night, Abby."

"Good night, Daddy."

And as he walked back to the living room, he'd invariably hear her again.

"Juice please, Daddy."

He'd fill her sippy cup with water and a splash of orange juice and go quietly back into her room. If he took a bit longer to return, he would sometimes find her already asleep, tucked in with her favorite blanket. Keith wasn't sure, but Sam might have actually knitted that blanket for her third daughter. A few years before, that same blanket had been by Abby's side regardless of the time of day or night. She had tickled her nose with the small frill on the sides as she lay in her crib, waiting patiently for someone to come get her until she learned to knowingly call out to whoever had put her to bed the night before, as if the bond with that parent was strengthened with every tucking, every bottle of milk brought, every "Nightie night" exchanged.

Looking down at his daughter as she slept, Keith invariably thought the amazing peace and purity embodied in a sleeping child was one of the greatest gifts God could give. It was a ritual as old as time, and it amazed Keith, as it had his ancestors and theirs before them, the power a child held to bring out the best in people.

As he stood outside his truck, he looked up at the sky and thought that God had betrayed him. Not that he was very religious, but he wanted someone to blame, someone to hate, and God seemed like a good and worthy target for his rage. He felt that everything he believed in was absolutely pointless. The sky was blue and the sun shined although the day remained chilly on this January morning. Years later it gave him a profound sense of anger that a day as gorgeous as this one had become the saddest day of his life.

It would take him years to regain a sense of self even moderately comparable to the self-assured manner he had possessed before. And that former sense was not the result of wealth, great looks, unfathomable luck, or detestable arrogance. It was the simple conviction that he was a decent man who had been blessed with a wonderful wife, great stepdaughters, and the most precious daughter any man could wish for.

The day his life broke, Keith knew that someday a new life would begin but that it would require a tremendous amount of learning, a tremendous amount of healing. In the meantime, he had to get up every morning and go to work and pretend nothing had happened. During this time in his life, there was seldom a day that he didn't relive the aftermath of hidden truths and shattered convictions.

Keith had always considered marriage to be the most important decision you could make. There was a finality to it that overshadowed its potential fragility. Like the tattered blanket a child carries around, relationships with spouses might seem threadbare at times, but this was exactly why they were so comforting. In the familiarity, he found solace from the everyday, mundane activities that filled his days with tedium and insignificance. It was in his loved ones that he found validation and a sense of purpose.

Keith stood bravely and perhaps innocently before Sam, asking her not to leave, to give this simple life of theirs its time. He heard her harsh words and saw her harsher actions, but still he believed that the sum of their days together would guide her to the irrefutable fact that her life was by his side, that together they were the people they were meant to be. But Sam simply walked out, without a word, without a tear, without a farewell.

Sadness overcame Keith and washed him in its cold waters, leaving nothing in its passing but a quiet numbness, an unshakeable paralysis. It was as if he'd discovered he was unable to move his limbs. But was it that he couldn't move? Or was he too scared to try?

The divorce was the answer few foresee yet many find. As divorces go, theirs was neither the most bitter nor the most cordial. It fell naturally into the wastelands of divorces, that vast land where failed marriages lie strewn about, discoloring with time, showing their pathetic innocence and pettiness. In this putrid field, buried alongside memories, love stories were obliterated, and his was no exception.

A few months after Sam left, he began to bitterly suspect she had only wanted her green card and her children's green cards, which they all had obtained through marriage to him. Keith decided he had been an easy mark.

Sadness grew in Keith as inevitably as a thread that is pulled until it unravels the entire fabric. In his case, it wasn't that the fabric had worn through or been stained. It was that the fabric had been irrevocably lost and ceased to be. As if it had never been.

This feeling of despair came from deep within. It was a scream that never caught its wavelength and thus could never be heard. It was a silent scream asked by many before him and many after. It was the scream of *why?* As if any answer could be better than the brutal, cruel absence of one.

The sadness came also from a feeling of not belonging to Sam anymore, as if her warmth had provided his true home, as if in her embrace he had the tangible proof that he was part of something more, something better.

Sam had been an impeccable and bright parenthesis, the pause in his journey that had given him a reason to be the man he dreamed of being. And his reason was now gone.

Chapter 11

For Keith, the memories of his daughter's early years were inextricably intertwined with his memories of life with Samantha.

As Abby grew a bit older, she realized something had happened between her parents that caused their divorce and left a cold void. Her father seldom mentioned her mother, and her mother seldom mentioned her father, but she could feel the tension when they spoke, when they occasionally met at her school or at soccer practices or ballet recitals. This was not the segregation natural of a divorce but more an irrational attempt to abolish the other's existence and influence.

Abby cried many times as her father's animosity toward her mother crept into his attitude toward her, yet Abby always heard him say what a great mother Sam was and how proud she should be to be as beautiful as her. It was extremely hurtful to see her father play this contradictory, conflicting, and angry role over the years.

To her, their relationship was immaterial. She loved both her parents. She had many classmates whose parents were separated or divorced and took it in stride, yet she never sensed that her friends felt this uncomfortable territory of mutual antagonism between their parents that she felt between her own mother and father.

But Abby never revealed these feelings and thoughts to Keith. Like daughter, like father. Lips sealed. Revealing very little. Private to a fault.

It all came to a head when Abby was sixteen and she and Keith got into one of the most violent, bitter arguments they had ever had. Sure, a few arguments come with the territory of adolescence, but never had one escalated to the brutality of that evening. Neither could remember what triggered it, but it was a horrible evening for father and daughter alike. Perhaps it started after dinner when Abby wanted to drive to her mom's and Keith said no.

"It's a bit late, isn't it?"

"It's only 9:00," Abby said casually as she finished clearing the counter after their late dinner.

"Just call her. She's probably not even home."

"You wouldn't know," she said as she started to look for her car keys around the kitchen. "Have you seen my car keys?"

"It's really late for you to be driving across town."

"So, you want me to *not* see my mom? Why don't you come out and say it?"

"That's not what I said, Abb."

"I'm sensing that there's another motive here for not wanting me to leave."

"I want you to appreciate what I do for you a bit more and not run to her as often as you do."

"I'm not running anywhere, Dad. I just want to talk to her. And don't look at me like that!"

"I just wish..." Keith was uncertain of what to say.

"Do you think it's a competition, Dad? Do you want me to hate Mom so I can love you more? Is that your plan, Dad?"

"Hey, take it easy, Abb."

"It doesn't work that way."

"I certainly don't want you to hate your mother. I've always told you how much she loves you, but in my eyes, she doesn't deserve you, Abby. She never has. I'm sorry, but I can't change the way I feel. I know I shouldn't have said that, but I did."

"Yes. You shouldn't have. What a horrible thing to say! I can't believe you'd say something like that. You, of all people. As if it isn't enough what Aunt Rose and Emma say about Mom. Even Andrea. Besides, it's not for you to decide." Abby's voice gradually rose as tears came to her eyes.

Keith hated himself for hurting her, but this subject was ever present, dancing in their thoughts and now surfacing with barely concealed bitterness.

"After the years I spent with Mom," Abby said, her voice shaking, "I moved in with you because I love you. But I won't let you decide what my relationship with my mother should be. You have no right, Dad."

"All I'm trying to do is tell you that you really don't know who she is. What she is. You're blind. She has lied to you for years about our marriage."

"And you think you know her, Dad? You haven't spoken to her in what? Ten years? You don't even dare look her in the eye. You think I'm stupid and don't notice how you change when you've seen her? You become someone else. Cold. Distant. And I don't like you. That's not you. Or is it? You know nothing about her."

"All I need to know is that she's the most selfish woman I've ever known, and I don't want you to become that. You are far better than she ever will be. What has she taught you, Abb? What? You're smart and independent, but above all you have a kindness she doesn't even comprehend. Your mother has many wonderful qualities, but those aren't it. Being pretty is not enough in this world, Abb. I hope I've taught you better."

"I'll become what I want, Dad. It's my choice." Abby's eyes were now half closed, accusing, searching for the weak links in his armor.

"Abby, you're sixteen years old, and, no, you will not become whatever you want."

"So everything you've said is bullshit? Like telling me that I can be whatever I dream of? Has it all been a lie, Dad? Another one of your goddamn lies? Beautiful words for a book that nobody reads? Lies!" she taunted her father, both now throwing wounding words at each other.

"Watch your language, Abb. And you know there are better examples to follow."

"Who? You? Dad, I haven't seen you do anything for me lately. Or for yourself, for that matter. You work. Come home. Open a tequila bottle. Go to bed. You haven't cooked a meal in months. I don't know where my father went. You don't play your guitars, you haven't published an article in forever. You used to smile all the time. What happened? Why are you so goddamn bitter?"

"Well, maybe I haven't done anything for you because you're never home anymore. And just a friendly reminder that the car you drive, the clothes you wear, and the trips you take, I pay for. I work my ass off to give you a pretty decent life. Don't learn the ingratitude of your mother, Abby. That's not you. But lately, everything is more important than being home. God, you've finally become the obnoxious teen I knew you would. And I'm fine with that because I trust you, but don't let that screw up your future. I saw your grades and they're slipping. You can't do that, Abby, not in your junior year. Keep up your end of the bargain."

"My grades are slipping, Dad? Is that what you call it when I get all As and one fucking B?

"I said watch your language, Abby!" Unable to control himself, Keith hit the kitchen counter with a force that scared her.

They had never gotten so angry at each other. Ever. As Keith recognized the fury of her mother being replicated in this passionate young woman, he was torn between her strong stance and his need to remain in control. He was surprised by this show of emotion from her yet inexplicably threatened.

"I learned that language from you, Dad, not from my mother."

"Oh, so, you want to be her instead of me? Is that it, Abby? Then learn to be her well!" Keith's voice now rose in anger. "Look at what your mother did. All the privilege, all the opportunities, and yet she barely finished high school. She did nothing with her life! Learn from her mistakes and from mine. Make yourself the best future possible. It won't happen if you learn to drop out of high school, too. Say the hell with Stanford or any other great school. Learn how to always depend on others. Who's going to support you then? Your mom? Her husband? What is it now? Her fourth? I've heard that one before! Are you going to work at Walmart, kid? Your mother couldn't even support her two daughters. The only reason she came to me was because she had lost all her money and I was kind enough or stupid enough to take her and her kids. Who do you think helped them? Emma and Andrea's father? I did. Always. Why don't you ask your mother?"

"Shut up, Daddy! Shut up!" Abby screamed.

"You want to be her? Then learn to cheat on those who love you, Abby. Have your mother tell you the truth about herself for once in her fucking life."

"Nice going, Dad, very proper and eloquent language! There's a lady right here, remember? What happened to all the fancy words, eh, Dad?"

"This is my house and I'll say what I want when I want. Are we *fucking* clear?"

They were both breathing hard and shaking, staring at each other in anger.

"Why the hell do you think you live here?" Keith continued. "Because, like it or not, I'm the one who gives a shit. I always have, and you know it! And yes, I push you and push you and push you. I've been doing it since you were born. And I'm not going to stop now. If I do it, it's because I've never stopped believing in you. And because getting good grades is easy, but getting the best grades takes a lot of effort. And it will open lots of doors for you. Don't throw it all away, Abby. You've worked too hard all these years. Don't be like your mother, always wait-ing for someone to rescue her."

"Am I going to be like you, then? Is that what you really want? Someone who's let his routines become his life? Who reads his books and lives the lives of others? What about your life, Dad? It doesn't look too good these days. Have you ever stopped and asked me what I want? What I like? All you care about is where I go to school, and that's not everything, Dad. What if I don't want to go to school? Maybe I just want to travel. Or do nothing for a while. There is a life I have to live, and it's not going to be the one you choose for me."

They both looked at each other, measuring the hurt, deciding whether to attack or seek a truce. Keith decided on the latter.

"You're missing the point, Abby," he finally said. "It's not about a school or about grades. It's about integrity. It's about your dreams."

"You know nothing about my dreams," she hissed.

"Maybe you're right. I don't know about your dreams." Keith softened his tone, wanting to extricate himself, extricate *them*, from this free fall, from the bitterness that had captured them. "Tell me about your dreams. Let me in, Abby."

But Abby was not giving up. Her anger and her youth mixed in her impetus to be right, to not be defeated.

"There's one thing Mom's always done better than you, Dad, and that's know how to enjoy life."

"That might be true. So what else have I been so bad at? Get it all out, Abby!"

"Now *you're* missing the point. Mom has lived life to the fullest. Something you clearly haven't."

"*To the fullest* might mean different things to different people. But be my guest and go and enjoy life with her."

"Maybe I will."

"No *maybes* Abby. You want to move out and go to your mother?" Keith was losing control again. "Just keep in mind that all those pretty clothes from Neiman's hanging in your closet and your shiny little car in the driveway, they all stay here. You decide." Keith knew he had gone too far, but he couldn't stop himself. He couldn't keep from trying to control her.

"Fine. Keep all your shit. I don't want it. I don't care!" Abby walked toward the door but then turned, her face contorted with raw anger.

"Let me ask you one thing, Dad. If you really think she's such a horrible person, then explain to me why you've been waiting for her to come back home for the last thirteen years. Why do you still keep her picture in your wallet? Did you think I never saw it?"

There was no turning back now.

"How many times have I seen you looking at her pictures. Playing her favorite songs after you've finished your bottle of tequila or whatever you're drinking on any given night. I've seen you reading her letters. I'm not stupid. Thirteen years of waiting. It's really sad, pure and simple."

She knew she had hit a raw nerve. "So, why, Dad? Why?" she pushed on. She knew she could win this.

Keith stood speechless.

"Did you ever give her one good reason to come back to you? You know the answer to that. Deep down, you know the answer. Maybe you didn't deserve her. Have you thought of that, Dad? Maybe that's exactly why she couldn't stand you, because you simply wanted to let life pass you by. And she certainly didn't. Maybe that's why she left you. And it's time you finally realize she's never, never coming back. Ever."

Abby slammed the front door as she walked into the rain, leaving Keith drained and defeated in the kitchen. And slowly the shadows grew longer and the night descended on the anguish and sadness that filled their home that evening.

Keith continued, dazed, down the tunnel of memories of his daughter and all the years of raising her. Although there was undeniably pain, he relived these memories with an honesty he hadn't been able to find in the more than twenty years since those events had taken place. He saw the string of facts more completely and didn't shirk from the sharp edges he'd avoided for years.

Now the floodgates were open, and Keith finally sat at a sidewalk café in the July sunshine, emboldened, ready to face the memories that had been his albatross and weighed him down year after year. Maybe it was the free spirit that Jay's arrival brought out in him. Even if he was mistaken and it was something else, it served to propel him through this cathartic journey and its maze of streets with their honking and smoke and urban insanity.

He remembered the afternoon Abby had called to tell him her mom had suffered a mild stroke. Crying, she'd told him Sam was in a hospital in Mexico City.

Without hesitation, Keith had packed a small bag, told some people at the office that he had a family emergency, and headed to the DFW airport, where he'd jumped on a late afternoon flight.

That same evening, he was at Sam's side. He walked into her room and was surprised that no one was present. Not her current boyfriend, any friends, or even one of the girls.

Samantha lay sleeping, her breath even and deep.

He moved closer to her side and realized that the glowing, suntanned skin of years ago had become blue and translucent on Sam's chest and arms. The strong arms he had been convinced he'd die in had lost their strength and now looked thick and flabby. The strong shoulders of her youth had given way to pale, spotted slopes on which her hair, perfectly combed, rested.

In the fifteen years since he'd last seen her, she had aged. Her face had wrinkles he hadn't expected, but behind the years, she remained breathtakingly beautiful.

He looked at her closely as he took her hand. Under the freckles, he could still see the fine features of the girl he had gazed at more than fifty years earlier: the small, sculpted nose, the full lips, the slight wrinkle in her brow, which had deepened with the years and which she had fought fiercely with cream and sunscreen since she was a young woman.

There was the almost imperceptible small scar above her lip from a fall when she was nine and had lost control of her bicycle on a dusty road so long ago.

"Why did you come, Keith?" she suddenly asked, startling him as he stared again into the ocean of her eyes, unchanged in their luster and intensity.

Once again, as he had all those years before, he was tilted off course by her voice. As the dusk outside leaked into the quiet room, Keith went ahead and said the words he'd held back for almost twenty years.

"I don't know exactly why. But I'm sure you know…you've always known, haven't you? All I could think of as I sat on the plane earlier today was that this time can be part of the better part. In this dusk of our lives, there is still room for a dream, our dream, the one we never thought would come true. The one we never quite finished living, Sam. The time we dreamed of is here. It is in my awe at holding your hand and knowing that this is life. And although life is good for me, it was always better in the places and times we spent beside each other. It's still my dream to hold your hand and look at the horizon and be convinced that there is another day for us, a new beginning."

He paused heavily. "It's never too late, Sam. It's never too late."

Her eyes were closed and he wasn't sure she had heard him, but then a few tears slipped down her face as she gradually drifted into a deep sleep, and Keith knew she had heard every word.

Keith continued to hold her hand, cherishing the moment and lamenting the years they could have shared but hadn't.

He also thought that when she woke, she finally would say what a mistake she'd made in leaving a good husband, a good friend, a good father. But those words were never to come from Sam's lips, not then, not ever.

Night fell on the city as he held her hand with tenderness. When she woke, she was in a haze and seemed unaware of where she was and who Keith was. After a few moments, recognition came to her eyes. She took his hand firmly and placed it on her heart. He was unsure what she was about to do or say. He held his breath.

She opened her eyes and said ever so softly, "Please don't say more, Keith. Time has passed. A lifetime has passed. Don't ever doubt that I once loved you, because I did. With all my heart. But we wanted different things from life. Don't ever doubt my girls loved you, because they did and still do."

She rested for a minute, breathing heavily, for once thinking carefully what to say.

"But now, please leave. Let go, Keith. Live the life you have before you. I know it will be a good life. Find someone who loves you just the way you are. And always take care of Abby. You've been a good father to her. Don't lose her as you did me. And take care of my girls, too, because you made them part of you. At least you did long ago. Don't let them down. Don't shut them out anymore. They deserve better."

She let go of his hand.

He knew her well enough to know that in spite of the softness in her voice, there was a steel undercurrent. He had forgotten what it did to him. He hadn't felt so rejected, so naked, since the day he'd learned she was having an affair.

He picked up his small backpack, but before he left the room, he turned and said, "I thought I might not ever see you again."

She opened her eyes and looked straight into Keith's eyes with the defiant look and stance he had long forgotten. To his shock and dismay, he saw what looked like hatred in her eyes.

Keith managed to control his voice. He would never allow her to a see a tear from him. She had seen him cry many years ago, broken by her vicious words, and she had smiled in victory.

Never again would that happen, he had vowed, yet here he was.

"I worried. That's why I came. I guess I never learned how to stop thinking...worrying about you. I never once stopped hoping that maybe one day you would need me...If you had only known that my door stayed open for you always. That's what stayed with me all those years."

"You're wrong, Keith. Sometimes it's too late to go back, and besides, nothing stays behind. Nobody stays behind. Except those who want to." Her tone revealed the harshness she had always possessed, right below the surface, simmering.

"Why all the hatred, all the bitterness, Sam? What did I ever do to you except love you, love your children?"

This was what he *wanted* to say, but she had closed her eyes, perhaps drifted off to sleep, and words mattered no more to her. So those words, those questions, remained forever unspoken.

In the taxicab as he returned to the Mexico City airport that night, Keith fell upon the realization that there was a transient essence to his relationship with Sam that had always been there.

He had blamed her for their failed marriage, specifically for her affairs, when instead he should have realized long ago that their love had simply outgrown its purpose.

And that purpose was the strong and driving force to reconnect them to their shared past. They were in their early thirties when they reconnected at that restaurant long ago, both in relationships that were ending, both tired of the monotony of their daily routines.

Sam's routines were comprised of the seemingly endless social engagements that distanced her from her first marriage and her children. The game of marriage had lost its glamour, and the financial wealth she had anticipated had gradually been depleted by her ex-husband's lack of business acumen as well as by her own lack of commitment to the hard work that a successful business requires.

The dullness of Keith's routines eventually compelled him to conclude that his early professional success wasn't all that it was cracked up to be. He had a nice car, a decent place to live, and even a few Armani suits, but even with all those things in place, empty and alone, he drank himself into unconsciousness every Friday and Saturday night and sometimes in between.

In the process, he alienated one or two good women who simply wanted to be loved.

That was the context of the two worlds that collided that Saturday afternoon at the Italian restaurant where Keith and Sam had their first date. It was a simple glimpse into their past that ended in a tornado of emotions. Ironically, it proved to be a look into their future, but they didn't look closely enough to recognize it.

As the streets of Cuernavaca faded into shadows of early afternoon, the vividness of Keith's memories grew. As he often did, he made mental notes of this reminiscing so that he could commit it all to paper in a story.

As a young man, he hadn't known he would write something anyone would read, but that changed when Abby turned five and he wrote an article for a magazine he occasionally freelanced for. The simplicity of the piece had been a hit with readers and had opened doors for him with bigger magazines and as a writer of short stories years later.

Although he made his living as a designer and his love for music was ever present, he always felt in his heart that he was a crafter of words.

After that article was published, he began writing in earnest and found a new path he traveled for years. When Abby was thirteen, he published his first book. But the piece he wrote for and about Abby remained a personal favorite.

My Life with Abby: A Brief Story of the Greatest Gift in a Small Package

Like any other five-year-old, Abby is a bundle of rambunctious and imagination-fueled activity. She runs with purpose and confidence at all times, looking at the world and wanting to learn and be part of everything in it. And just as she can swim for hours in a pool with imaginary sharks and mermaids, she can sit quietly in her room playing with her dolls in a world of her own. But it isn't only dressing and undressing them that keeps her enthralled most afternoons. It's the amazing tales she weaves that keep her going. She gives these little people names and establishes traits and qualities for each one. Just as she talks to them and about them, she also makes them talk amongst themselves. Friendships are forged as these little people become BFFs and play in a way that many of us have sadly long forgotten. Meanwhile, a little miracle of imagination takes place right before my eyes.

But Abby makes little miracles happen throughout the day. They happen when she's telling me she wants to be an artist and draws picture after picture of trees and flowers and of her mommy and volcanoes and kites. They happen when she's playing with her rock collection and decisively tells me that she's going to be a geologist, even if we both admit that we're not quite sure what a geologist does. But it doesn't really matter, because the next day she's off and running to new dreams. That day she wants to be a cheerleader, and the next day a singer, and the next day a ballerina.

Of course, there are costumes, and it must be in her genetic makeup to be a princess, because it's clear that every five-year-old across America and beyond finds no greater bliss than in playing dress up. I'd never take away from Disney, but even without Belle and Jasmine and Snow White, I'd bet money that little girls would still find the path to imaginary lands with evil witches, handsome princes, and strange fairies with unicorns by their sides, lands over which my Abby, and every little girl, rules supreme. And when I call to tell her that dinner is ready, in walks none other than Cinderella in full blue regalia: gloves, tiara, and all. Another miracle takes place right there, in our dining room no less.

My life with Abby is an endless source of joyous and unscripted stories that unfold at every turn. And, as much as I take care of her, she somehow knows that she takes care of me as well. And she does a phenomenal job. We love each other without end and learn from each other without end.

But it seems a little one-sided at times, as if one of us is learning so much more from the other. I say this because as I've taught her to love everything from great food to Vivaldi, she has taught me to be a better human being. Every day. While I have taught her to sit up straight and say "Yes ma'am" and "Thank you," she has taught me to believe in fairytales once again.

As I have taught her to ride her bike without training wheels, shown her the beauty in flowers, and told her the tragedy of the Titanic endless times, she has taught me to dream a little bit more, to laugh a little bit more, to love life a whole lot more.

So, as I glance at her in my rearview mirror on our way to school each morning, singing Hannah Montana with unbridled zest at this early hour, I realize that, as much as I thought I'd given life to this amazing little surprise that God gave me, what took place was exactly the opposite. So thank you, Abby, for giving life to this guy who was given the gift of being your dad.

———————◆◆◆◆◆◆◆◆◆———————

He had cut out the article "My Life with Abby" and given it to his daughter along with a pair of diamond earrings on her seventeenth birthday. As they sat that evening in the courtyard restaurant of the Four Seasons in Mexico City, sharing a bottle of wine, tears rolled down her cheeks.

"Thanks, Daddy. It's beautiful. And the earrings are gorgeous. Thank you for everything."

"Quite the contrary, Abb; thank you. My life changed forever when I found out you were on the way. It's that simple and irrefutable. Your mom and I both made many mistakes, but we did one thing together superbly, and it was having you, ladybug."

"Why does it sound so familiar? As if I've seen or heard those words before."

"The story?"

"Yes. I've heard it before."

"I used to read it to you when you were little. You even tried to read it yourself. Then it just got put in a box and forgotten. I hoped that one day we'd have a chance to read it together, sometime when you could really understand what it meant to see you grow up. One day I looked for it and couldn't find it. I looked in old boxes, between the pages of old books, and in some old computer files I'd archived. Finally I found it, along with some other things. There's a box we used to throw things into when you were little. It was there at the bottom."

"Our forever box," Abby said without thinking. "I'd forgotten all about it. How could I, Dad?"

"You named it. One day you came up to me and said, 'Daddy, can you get our forever box down?'"

"I said, 'What forever box, Abby?' and you pointed to the box in the closet where we used to put your stuff. And I understood that for you the things we put in there would be there forever. You chose each item carefully. It was the right name."

"Somehow I lost track of it."

"Well, you became a teenager one moment and a woman the next. And kids want to distance themselves from their parents and their childhoods. It just happens. That's precisely why I kept it. So that one day you'd find it and find yourself in it."

"And?" she said softly, anticipating the words that would follow. She knew her father's way of moving with ease between moods and words.

Keith paused as he found the words with which he made her past come true. "Well, in finding the box, I remembered a bunch of moments that feel so far away I have to wonder if they were once real."

He looked at his daughter and saw a new anticipation in her eyes he hadn't seen in a while, so he continued. "I remember one day in the middle of winter, I came home from work and your mother had dinner ready and the fireplace going. We lived in Dallas back then. You were probably about two. When you heard the door open, you came running, yelling *Daaaaaaaaddyyyy!* and rushed into my arms. I kissed you, then I kissed your mom, and then I kissed your sisters as we sat at the table."

He paused for a moment, closing his eyes so that every vivid memory was called upon and relayed to his daughter.

"I'm not sure why, but that was one of the most wonderful days in my life. I remember your mother's perfume, something from Prada she used to wear, leaving a wonderful wake as she passed by, and her smile as I walked in, the smell of her favorite chicken recipe coming from the kitchen, the soft steps of your sisters coming down the stairs to dinner, and the sound of your tiny boots on the kitchen tile. As much as other memories have faded, I remember that day like it was yesterday. Your mother looked so happy. I've always wondered where we went wrong, where I went wrong."

"You did nothing wrong. Life happens, Dad. We know that well."

And as they raised their glasses to toast, she concluded, "To us."

"To us, Miss Abby."

They sat in silence for a while, Keith reminiscing about how he had always loved the way they could share stories and engage in great conversations. Ever since she was a tiny little girl sitting in the back seat of his car, he could always count on endless stories and questions or her loud singing as she listed to her little pink iPod.

He was always amazed by all the words that came from the minuscule chatterbox strapped to the booster seat behind him.

But they also shared the silences.

If there was one thing he was never able to share with Emma and Andrea, it was silence. They were all at a loss when silence overtook the mood and crept into dinner or a long drive home. In that regard, they were so like their mother, as if life would be wasted without sound, words, and laughter.

But Abby had intuitively decoded her father's love for brooding, quiet afternoons spent listening to the wind or a cello partita.

Chapter 11

They had often sat by the sea over the years, and Keith had taught her to respect it and to be amazed by its immensity. Young as she was, Abby could always sit in silence for a few minutes taking in the horizon, the clouds, and the flocks of seagulls above. Until, of course, the four-year-old took over and she ran to the incoming sea, yelling with a happiness that came from deep within a child's imagination and heart. At moments like that, Keith had felt complete.

"I have some news to share with you, Dad." Abby looked up at him with a brightness in her eyes and an eagerness in her voice that brought Keith back to the moment and the grown daughter sitting in front of him. He wondered, not for the first time, when she had stopped being a sweet little girl and had become this beautiful woman.

He looked intently into her face, trying to read a sign, a *travesura* in the making, a worry.

"You'd better not be pregnant, young lady. I'll have to kill the son of a bitch," he answered, attempting for some levity.

"Funny." She smiled briefly and then became serious.

He sensed her nervousness.

"It's something we talked about a long time ago. Something I've been waiting for. And so have you."

"Is it about school?" he ventured, equally nervous now.

She nodded.

"You got the letter. You were accepted."

He didn't even have to name the school he had dreamed she'd attend one day. Since she was very young, he had instilled in her the quest to make it into a top college. Today, she was making one of his life's wishes come true.

She reached to her purse on the backrest of the chair, pulled out a letter, and placed it on the table in front of him.

He took his glass and drank, hiding the emotion welling in his eyes.

"I never doubted you'd make it. Okay, maybe once in a while I doubted it a bit. Am I a terrible father to admit that?"

"No, you're not a terrible father." She paused.

"Really?"

"Okay, just a little terrible. But I forgive you, old man."

"Oh, so now you're the one who has to forgive me?" he teased. Keith looked at his daughter and saw the little girl of fifteen years ago. She was unmistakable with her slightly raspy voice, just like her mother's. His baby girl, always singing, always a bit off key, always a bit too loud.

Her words brought him back to the present.

"You haven't even read the letter," she said, moving the paper closer to him. Her brown eyes were pools of excitement, anticipation, and pride.

Keith looked down at the white sheet of paper in front of him but didn't pick it up. He saw the name of the school on the envelope and slid it back to her side of the table.

"I don't have to, Abby. I know what it says."

"How do you know, Dad?"

"Have you forgotten? It's my job, Miss Abby."

He felt incredible pride in this young woman sitting before him with the stunning face that so resembled her mother at that age. Keith had not been with Sam as a young woman, but he had seen the surprisingly few photos her own mother had kept of her. Abby possessed a thinness her mother had never had. Sam was a stunning woman but had a power in her body her third daughter had not inherited. Still, there was a fullness in Abby's hips Sam had lacked.

Grown as she was, it amazed him that she still inadvertently sought his approval.

"Congratulations, Abby. I am so proud of you."

"Thanks. I'm pretty proud myself."

"You should be. Have you told your mother?"

"She doesn't know yet. I wanted you to be the first to know."

At that, Keith's pride swelled even higher, fuller. The simple gesture meant so much.

"Please call her after dinner. She'll be extremely proud. Just as I am."

He tried to cover his tears, and she tried to cover hers.

"Don't get all mushy on me, Dad..."

"Who? Me?" But it was hard to contain the tears that welled up. "Well, my daughter being accepted to such a great school clearly deserves another bottle," he declared as he called the waiter, signaling for another bottle of the Monte Xanic Cabernet he was so fond of.

"I think I've had too much wine already. You, too, but go ahead," she said, knowing full well how much this letter meant to her father.

"Have I not taught you well, young lady? There is no such thing as too much wine."

The evening was beautiful. They had met here in this city of over twenty million people, Abby visiting friends and Keith visiting old business partners and secretly hoping to see his daughter.

The courtyard of the Four Seasons in Mexico City, off Reforma Boulevard, was as stunning as it had been when Keith had brought Abby to visit when she was so young he had to order a crib for their room.

"God! Time goes by so fast."

Then there was silence as father and daughter took in the evening, the water splashing in the center fountain as the only backdrop along with a murmur of the city bustling outside those walls.

After a few minutes, the waiter arrived with a bottle that, to Abby's surprise, wasn't the dark bottle of her father's favorite wine but the deep green color of a familiar brand of champagne that was opened with mastery and a pop that immediately became the liquid flow spilling into the two flutes set in front of them.

They raised their glasses and toasted.

"I've waited a long time for this, my dear."

"Well, Dad, for the most part you've kept your promises. I thought I should keep mine as well. You do know how much effort getting this letter took? How many nights I had to stay home and study instead of going out with my friends? The parties I missed? The boys who lost interest! You were an evil man enslaving your daughter. Making me stay home and study."

"Yes, you poor sweet girl, living such a hard life!" he said with a smile.

"We'll see how this first semester goes. What if I'm not good enough?"

"Then you can go to community college and I can save tons of money."

"Dad!"

"I'm teasing you, Abb. You're going to be fine. You'll have to work hard, but it will be worthwhile."

"I sure hope so, Dad."

"So, how does it feel, Abb?" He looked her straight in the eye.

"It feels freaking great, Daddy," she replied with a huge proud grin on her face.

"Sometimes there are angles, gestures, that make you look just like your mother," Keith suddenly remarked. "It's uncanny. But you are more beautiful."

"Ahh, Dad, you're sweet. But I've seen Mom's photos of when she was young. She was stunning. She still is. I've never been *that* beautiful."

"To me you are. Always have been and always will be."

Silence then visited them again, but it wasn't a silence of uneasiness, of urgent thoughts racing to find words.

It was more the old, well-worn silence of this odd pair: the older man who hid his loneliness behind the symmetry of his life and his beloved daughter, a grown woman now eager to fly and the greatest surprise life had ever given Keith.

⸻ ◆◆◆◆◆◆◆◆◆ ⸻

The brief episodes Keith was exploring came and went without rhyme or reason but were acutely centered on memories of his beloved daughter. After all, she had been Keith's companion for such a long time.

As he reached the Cuernavaca cathedral that afternoon, he thought back to weddings past. He sat on a bench inside the cathedral grounds and, once again, the present day, this July 10, stood still as prior years came rushing back.

In remembering weddings, Abby's came to mind.

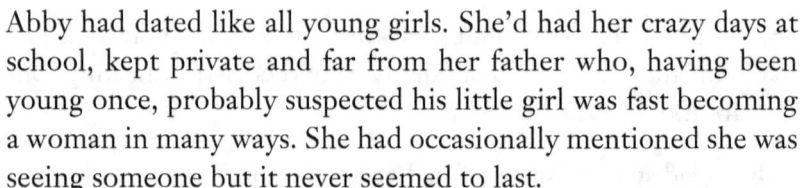

Abby had dated like all young girls. She'd had her crazy days at school, kept private and far from her father who, having been young once, probably suspected his little girl was fast becoming a woman in many ways. She had occasionally mentioned she was seeing someone but it never seemed to last.

She had eventually introduced Thomas Robinson to her father. He was a smart young architect she had met during her grad school years at SMU, having returned to Dallas a few years after her undergrad at Stanford. They were both twenty-seven when they met.

Keith had liked Thomas on the spot. He was a good-looking young man with short brown hair and eyes as blue as the tiles of a California pool. Although he'd never been overprotective of Abby, Keith had always been a bit nervous about her choice in boys, perhaps a legacy of his own failed relationships.

Thomas seemed confident and steady, and Keith had seen him look at his daughter with a tenderness that could not have been anything but honest and true. After a couple of years of dating, they came to him with the news that they were getting married.

A few years later, just a couple of days before her wedding, Abby had visited her father. They had sat outside on the terrace at his home to chat.

"There was a time, Abby, when you still asked me if I loved your mom. You were probably five or so. You asked...Actually, you demanded that we be together." Keith could see her in her booster seat, adamant, filled with conviction.

"As if by your mere will it would happen," he continued. "And, of course, I wanted that too, but I knew it would never happen. And I wanted to protect you from an expectation that would never be."

For the first time in her life, Abby asked a question she'd wondered for a long time. "Daddy, would you have stayed with mom if she had returned? Would you have opened the door if she'd come knocking?"

"There are two answers to that question. The simple one is a decisive *yes*. The second and better answer is that I've never known the answer, my dear. I did ask myself that question many times." Keith looked through the fog of some of those days twenty-some years ago.

"There was a part of me that said I would have, without a single question, without any accusation, blinded by my love for your mother all over again. But I knew that reality eventually would have reared its ugly head, maybe in the form of a simple disagreement that brought out the frustration, the anger. We were always so different. At first that was the attraction, but later, it drove us apart." After a pause, Keith continued.

"What I will tell you, my daughter, as you are a few days away from your own wedding, is that loving one person for a lifetime is possible. I never loved another woman like I loved your mom. She was the one. I know many people who believe that you have several true loves in a lifetime. They're entitled to their opinion; I'm entitled to mine."

Keith continued, "For years, I missed her at night when I reached to her side of the bed, always by the door, but found an empty space where she should have been warm and asleep. I missed her when you went off to college and I cleaned out your room.

I literally talked to her out loud as I packed up your dolls and games. I wanted someone to be my accomplice in keeping the memories held in your room. I wanted to tell her how brave she was the morning we headed to the hospital and you were born. She was calm and reassuring and told me everything would be okay. Our roles were reversed for a few hours. She was in charge then. She had done it all before with Andrea and with Emma, while I was a nervous wreck."

"I can't imagine Mr. Cool himself not being in control." Abby smiled, knowing that she had opened the floodgates to her father's river of memories.

"I missed her when I taught you how to ride your bike. We should have shared that moment, but she stole that from me, Abby. She should have been there to see you, scared at first as you realized you were on your own, pedaling, and then finding your balance. She should have been there when your fear gave way to pride and amazement, shouting '*Look at me, Daddy! Look at me!*' For some reason, I missed her so much that day."

Keith was lost in reverie. "She made us separate our lives with you. It wasn't the fact of our separation. What hurt was to see *your* life bisected as if it were two separate instances of parallel memories when I thought your life should have been a quilt of pieces of life shared as a family. I'm so sorry it worked out that way."

"We made it through, Dad. Sure, you'll have to pay for my therapy for the rest of your life, but we're okay," Abby teased.

"There were so many nights I imagined hearing a knock on the door. I would open the door and she would walk in to stay forever so that we could watch you grow up together. She stole that dream from me, from us, and she took your sisters from me. I know they're not my daughters, I know they never were, but I loved them just as much as I love you. I saw them grow and I saw

180

their mark on me and mine on them. And I loved that. I really missed Emma and Andrea. I still miss them."

"Mom didn't steal that from you, Dad. She didn't steal it from me, either. She gave me so much that you never saw, that you never asked about. You might refuse to believe it, but she was the greatest mom anyone could have had. I just wish I had told her that more often. "

It was Abby's turn to speak her point of view, to give her opinion with the conviction her parents had both instilled in her.

"You have everything a father could ever wish he had. You have great memories. You have, and *we* have, all the trips we took together, all the plays we saw over the years, all the concerts, plus all these memories not only of both of us but also of my sisters. Emma and Andrea adore you. To this day, the three of us always say that Emma is your favorite. I should feel awful but I don't because I see the love you always gave us, even if Emma and Andrea weren't your real daughters."

Abby experienced a flood of emotions herself as the conflicting feelings of her wedding came upon her.

"But don't blame Mom for everything. You could have married again, Daddy. You could have loved again. There were so many times when I hoped you would find someone like Mom did. Maybe too often, but that's another story...there was a time when you went out a lot. I saw women come and go. I was little, but I saw them, and I remember some of them. I guess in my child's mind, I knew you were looking for someone like Mom."

Naturally, without shame, Abby's tears fell like soft rain. "And then one day, I realized that it wasn't that you couldn't find someone to love; it was that you didn't *want* anyone else. I saw you write your beautiful stories, the newspaper articles, and one day I understood it was your anger, and sadness, that gave you the will to write with such heart. You needed a conflict to give your writing substance. You needed someone to blame. Mom just happened to be convenient."

"Maybe you're right, my dear."

"Come on, Dad! I've read every line, every poem, every short story you've written. And your writings are truly beautiful, Daddy, but you know what? It will always be better to live love, to experience it, to breathe it, even to be hurt by it, than to just write about it."

More tears came, and she dabbed at her eyes, those gorgeous brown eyes.

They both knew these were tears not of sadness but of the bitter-sweet truths and memories that entwined them.

"I know that now more than ever. I'm in love, Daddy. And I know you're happy for me. And that makes *me* happy. But I would love to see you in love one day. I know I'd be a bit jealous about some woman in your life, but it would make me very happy if you could feel again what I'm feeling this very moment. Don't give up, Dad." Then Abby softly recited,

No te salves.

No te llenes de calma.

No reserves del mundo sólo un rincón tranquilo.

No dejes caer los párpados pesados como juicios.

"You read that poem to me over and over again. I still remember it, every word. You were a pretty fucking weird father, pardon my French, reading poetry to me when I was so little! I had no idea what it meant. All I knew was that you found joy in the sound of those strange words. I guess I sensed they had some connection to us and our past, but now I understand them. I eventually did read Benedetti, believe it or not! Now it's up to you to show me, to prove to me, that you understand those lines as well. And the only way to do that is by living those words: *Don't be saved. Don't fill up with calm. Don't set aside just a peaceful corner of this world. Do not let your eyelids fall like judgments."*

"That's easy for you to say, Abb," Keith managed. "You have Thomas who loves you, who will marry you on Saturday. You had your mother. You've had me. Always loving you, always taking care of you. That has been the only thing I needed to be happy. I made a decision to make my life about you. I made some sacrifices, but I have no regrets. Look at you. You're a wonderful, smart, successful woman. I'd like to think I had something to do with who you are today. Now your beauty; that all comes from your momma. Sometimes I see you in certain angles, or you make a face that looks like your mother at your age, and it's just amazing."

"But I'm leaving, Daddy. I have my life to live, to travel, to make a home with Thomas, to one day have children who will drive us crazy. You taught me to find my way. And I have."

"And I am so happy, Abby. I'm so proud of you. And I'm proud of your sisters."

"Then be proud of yourself, Daddy. Of what you've done to help raise Mom's three children, two girls who were not yours but who love you without boundaries. Jesus, Dad, Emma looks more like you than I do. And you helped Mom raise me. She gave us things you didn't. She taught us things you couldn't. After all, we're chicks, Dad. You're a guy."

"Be proud of me too," Abby added, "of the good and the bad, because I'm not only your daughter when I get good grades and look pretty. I'm also your daughter when I cuss and when I fight and feel like shit and make mistakes and get my period and when I'm like my mom. I loved her so much," Abby reflected. "I always will. Sometimes I get the feeling that you wanted to compete against her for my love. That's not fair to anyone, Dad."

She seemed to wait for a reply from her father but none came.

"Let life be more important than order and parallel lines, Dad. Open your heart like you taught me to open mine. Find someone, Daddy. You deserve it. There's a very lucky woman out there waiting for you. Remember that poster that Jay gave you many years ago? The one that says '*Love is messy?*'"

He nodded.

"You know why I think you loved that poster? Because you were dying to feel what it would be like to be messy, to not worry, to open doors and let the leaves and the flies come in. You secretly wanted to play in the dirt all over again. So, what are you waiting for, Dad?"

"Abby, I'm sixty-nine. Do you really think I can start now? Do you really think there's some woman out there waiting for an old, bald man with a sagging ass who's set in his ways?"

They both laughed out loud.

"That's for you to find out, Old Man! But I'll keep my eyes open."

"Well, I'm not too sure. But, heck, I'll be on the lookout. Hell, I'm still a handsome son of a bitch."

"Dad, after all these years, I can assure you there are plenty of good women looking for a sweet man like you."

Abby and her father walked arm in arm back into the old house they still called home.

"I'm glad we talked, Daddy. I guess weddings just get us all emotional."

"Get some rest. We have a wedding on Saturday that I wouldn't miss for anything. I hear the bride will be even more beautiful than her mother. And that's hard to top, my dear. I'm even thinking of dancing a bit. Do you know if Thomas has a hot, slutty aunt I can chase around at your wedding?"

"Oh, Dad! You are incorrigible. You sound just like Jay. Just know that if you dance, I'll have to pretend I don't know you." Abby's eyes twinkled in the darkness. "By the way, when is Jay arriving? Thomas and I want to thank him. He sent yet another check a week ago to make sure we had all our wedding expenses covered."

"He's always loved pampering you. When all our friends would bring you little birthday gifts, Jay would send something utterly out of proportion. That's just Jay. He's been like that since we were kids. I walked into his house to play tennis the first time and an hour later he was giving me a $400 racket."

"I just can't see you as friends all these years."

"Lots of stories, my dear! Anyway, it's getting late. And please point out the skanky aunt at the wedding!"

"Get to bed, Dad. Just please keep your dancing to a minimum!"

"In some ways you are just like your mother. That sounds exactly like something she would say!"

Keith watched his daughter go up the stairs and then sat on the terrace. It would be nice to have someone to share life with. Solitude had been his companion long enough. It had just never quite happened. Maybe someday...

At the top of the stairs, Abby turned. "I know you might not want to hear this, Dad, but you have no idea how I wish Mom had lived to be here with me."

She never heard him reply softly to the night, "I do, too."

Keith could almost hear that conversation with Abby all those years ago. She had been so young yet so ready for the commitment and the expected magic of marriage.

Sitting at the sidewalk café now, in a silent celebration of his birthday, killing time before heading back home, Keith allowed his mind and heart to wander to that moment with his daughter. As the past was allowed to flow, his memories of her felt as warm and reassuring as the sun touching his face.

Chapter 12

Samantha Riley had not lived to see her youngest daughter get married. She was about to turn sixty-five when she passed away, six weeks before Abby's wedding. Abby had called Keith that morning in February.

"Dad? It's Abby."

He immediately sensed something in his daughter's tone. "Hi, my love. Is everything okay?"

He heard her crying and asked, "Abby, what's wrong?"

"Daddy, Mom died about half an hour ago." She said it slowly, as if afraid to feel more hurt than she already did, and also afraid to hurt her father with these words that needed to be shared between them.

"She never woke up. My sisters and I were with her. I thought you'd want to know. I held her hand. I thought of both of you. It should have been you holding her hand. God, Dad, you should have been with us."

Hearing the slightest hint of anger mixed with sadness, Keith remained silent.

"I'm sorry, Daddy." Abby began to cry.

Abby had used the familiar "my sisters." Every time she did, for just a fleeting moment, he wanted to correct her so she would say "my half sisters," but he never did. He knew it was shallow and beneath him to feel this way. Their love was too strong to be debated in technicalities, and even when it was awkward, he always respected the strong sense of sisters that Sam had instilled in them, regardless of their different fathers.

Abby continued to cry, and Keith wanted to hold his daughter, to tell her everything would be okay. He wanted to run to her side as he had when she was a child and tripped or fell off her bike.

But he could offer her no words. He felt numb and cold and unable to offer meaning or comfort.

Although Abby had told Keith a few months back that her mom was sick, he didn't realize how serious it was.

Over the years, daughter and father had developed a way of referring to Sam in tangential terms. Abby had always avoided talking too much about her life with her mother because, in doing so, she would need to talk about her mother's husband. After her mom's third divorce, there were other men, other boyfriends.

Keith knew that Sam didn't know how to live without a man. She had been raised to be dependent, to be rescued by someone, but he also knew there were things that were uncomfortable for Abby to hear, so he was always guarded when referring to her mom, hiding from her any unnecessary truths. They treaded lightly. By not asking, Keith had assumed that Sam's illness was not serious. He knew she had been diagnosed with skin cancer but had assumed it had been detected in time and that she would shrug it off.

He then recalled a conversation he'd had with Abby months before Sam's death, when she unexpectedly stopped by to visit one afternoon.

"Hi, sweetie, what a surprise."

"Hi, Dad. What are you doing?"

"Just fixing myself a little dinner."

"Keith, you don't know how to make a *little* dinner. So what is it? Molecular recipes? Five-course meal?"

"Are you making fun of me, young lady?" After she'd returned from college in California, she'd started calling him Keith. It felt a bit odd, but somehow he didn't dislike it.

"No, it's really a little nice, simple meal," he continued. "Pasta with clams and shrimp. Have you had dinner? There's plenty. And I just opened a bottle of nice wine."

"Let me think...Of course I do! I haven't had a good home-cooked meal in a while."

"Have a seat, ladybug. You timed it well." He immediately set an extra plate, delighted to see his daughter. God, how he missed her!

As they enjoyed the meal and the excellent wine, conversation flowed.

"I went to visit Mom, Daddy. She's been having a rough time. You should go see her."

"Go see her? Look, Abby, some exes remain friends, but your mom and I are old-fashioned. We just hate each other at a distance. We loved each other a long time ago and then we didn't. Simple as that. So the answer is *no*. Sorry. It's not my place."

"Can't say I didn't try," she said again, a bit lighter in tone.

"Yes, you did. Nice try by the way."

"Truth is, we think she's really sick. The doctor is doing some tests." Abby bit her lip.

"Sick, eh? Well, I could have told you that years ago," Keith tried to tease.

"It's not a joke. She's seriously ill. It could be cancer. Something in her skin," Abby said, her tone moving between anger and desperation.

Keith put down his glass and finally gave his daughter the attention she was asking for.

"Andrea told Emma and me she's been in and out of the hospital. We're really worried."

"Why tell me, Abb? Do you think I should care?" He regretted his words as soon as they left his mouth.

Abby's anger came swiftly. "Don't play the heartless bastard, Dad. You're not good at it. She's my mother and she used to be your wife. You could show some kindness."

"I do remember. And I hope she's okay. I'm sorry. It's just that...I'm not sure what you want me to do." He tried to ease the sudden tension between them.

"You don't have to do anything, Dad. Stop trying to always fix my world. I just wanted to talk to you, to be listened to. She's just suddenly looking old."

"Well, look at me, for crying out loud!"

"That's different. You're a guy. Sure, you're getting wrinkly and a bit chubby and what hair you still have has turned gray, but that's to be expected."

"That's nice to hear. Please don't hold back. Tell me how you *really* see me. Jesus!"

"You know what I mean. You look great. Mom always looked gorgeous but suddenly she's getting old. Brittle. You of all people should understand what it's doing to her. She fought hard, but time is taking its toll."

"Time always wins. It shows that she always felt those things wouldn't happen to her. As if time would pass her by."

"She doesn't say much, but she's lost a lot of weight and the three of us are worried. They'll know sometime this week. Andrea is with her."

"Abby, there's a time when you realize that your parents won't be with you forever. I went through that, too. It's really hard. It's a realization of your own mortality, of the inevitable."

"I just don't want to see her sick."

"Babe, she has taken great care of herself over the years, and she's as stubborn as you. Maybe even more so. So if she makes up her mind, she'll be fine. She loves to fight. Be there for her. That's all a mother can ask of her children. Plus, your wedding is in six months. I'll bet your mom will be there looking great, dancing the night away. That's what she does best. She always has!"

After Abby left, Keith thought back to when he'd rushed to Sam's side after her mild stroke. Afterwards, he'd felt like a fool for coming to her. He wasn't about to do that again.

The day Abby told Keith of Sam's passing, he felt deep sadness but also a fleeting moment of relief. He could finally say goodbye to Sam. More accurately, he could say farewell to the shadows she had cast for so long.

The silence on the line extended as each one of them, separated by many miles, saw the emptiness before them. They shared silence again, connecting as they always had. Then Abby spoke.

"Dad? Daddy, are you there? Did you hear me?"

"Yes, Abb. I did hear. I'm sorry. I know how much you loved your mother. She knew it too and always felt blessed by your love. You were always her baby girl. Always."

He heard her cry and cry. Unable to hold her, Keith ached. He didn't know what to say to his own daughter. She was the only person who knew that his love for her mom had never ever quite evaporated. As smart as she was, she must have wondered why and if what her father felt was true love.

He didn't know himself.

"Emma and Andrea will probably call you later, Dad," Abby finally said. "They've always liked a word of reassurance from you every now and then. Don't hide from them. If they haven't called by this afternoon, you might want to be the one to call them. You have their numbers. It would mean a lot to them...It would mean a lot to me, too."

Emma and Andrea's father had passed away some years back. Against all odds, Keith had remained a distant fatherly figure. Although both were married and had their own busy lives and children, they occasionally called to see how he was doing, and both had visited once or twice over the years.

Keith was always delighted to see them, and he always felt there was a little something of him in them. But once they left, he was always left with an emptiness he could only fill with alcohol and rage.

After all these years, there were days when he still missed Emma and Andrea. He had missed important dates in their lives. They had invited him to their college graduations and their weddings, yet he had not attended these occasions, feeling that seeing their mother would be another defeat.

When Sam left Keith and Keith moved away, Andrea had sought him out. She came to find answers her mother hadn't given her. This was his opportunity to show her that he would stand by her side, but Keith had turned his back on her. He had thought she was old enough to provide words of comfort to *him*, as if the care he had provided as she grew up needed to be paid back now in his time of need. Clouded by his own rage, he felt that being present for his stepdaughter would be a demonstration of love to a woman who didn't deserve it. He felt that continuing to love Andrea would concede yet another battle, would be a sign of weakness she would mock. So he left Andrea without answers, without words, without support in *her* time of need.

Years later, he sat with Andrea and apologized for not being there for her as he had been years before. Perhaps it was too late to matter or for her to care, but he regretted his behavior for the rest of his life. Telling her this opened a small window into each other's hearts that widened a bit more every time they spoke.

All the while, in the Christmas cards that came every year, Keith saw the differences between Andrea and Emma, glimpses into the women they had become. Andrea's cards came with a perfunctory message and a picture of her family made into a card at a corner Walgreens.

Emma's card was always accompanied by a beautiful letter much in the style Keith himself had used many years before in letters that told a little story about the family's adventures and anecdotes for the year. Even miles and years apart, the uncanny resemblances between Keith and his younger stepdaughter remained, mysteriously passed from one to the other during the years they had spent together. Even more than a physical coincidence, there were gestures, tones of voice, words that inextricably intertwined them.

Keith came back to the present. "Tell your sisters I love them. And take care of yourself, Abb. I miss you."

"I miss you too, Daddy. You have no idea how much. I'll call you once we make arrangements for the funeral." Before she hung up to tend to the dozens of details that had to be planned, she said, "Maybe you should come, Dad. You could say good-bye to her."

Absolute silence.

Over the years, Keith had sometimes been amazed at how well Abby knew him. It seemed that, as time went by, the tables had turned. He had known her so well when she was growing up. She had often been surprised at things he said and guessed about her. She'd shout in her little girl voice filled with awe and glee, "How did you know that, Daddy?"

And he'd always give her the same answer: "It's my job, Miss Abby."

He was taken aback now by his daughter's words because, at this moment, he was thinking that he wanted to go and join his daughter and his stepdaughters. This was a chance to be a family once again after so many years.

He had waited many years for a moment, a sign, that perhaps Sam had suffered a moment of self-doubt over her decision to leave him. With her death, she had robbed him of the chance to hear an admission that there had been times when she had cried at night, missing his embrace, missing the final chapter in the story they had set out to live.

His thoughts returned to his daughter. Unlike Emma and Andrea, Abby had inherited her mother's beauty. She had Sam's long legs, her hair, and that disarming smile that brightened the lives of those around her.

But Abby had a much more measured, cautious way about her that came from her father. Aside from his lips and his skin, she had also inherited long spells of silence and his meticulous way of doing everything, from writing her name to the care that always went into her school projects. Seldom was anything good enough for Abby.

Keith had never been to her office, but he imagined it was impeccable and organized, just as his had been all those years ago at the design firm where he had worked.

Keith smiled to himself, thinking how he must have driven Sam insane. To Sam, nothing had to be good or bad or so-so. To her, life was not about quality, measurements, or plans; it was simply about living.

Keith could imagine his daughter and stepdaughters huddled together, crying and missing their mom. Sam, after all, was bigger than life. She had filled the space around her with her incredible *joie-de-vivre*. She shined in a crowd and, without trying to, attracted others with her openness, her acceptance, and her trust. As she used to say, "I'm all heart." Even after discovering she had secrets like all human beings do, Keith still felt captive to her spell.

"I think I'll just stay here, Abby," Keith finally said. "I'm not sure I want to see all the people who will likely be there. But thanks for asking. When you and your sisters have a moment, call me and tell me where you'll lay your mom to rest."

He didn't plan to visit her gravesite. The bitter rage he'd once felt toward Sam had evaporated, but visiting her, even in death, seemed like another loss in their long-lasting battle. She was taking to her death the words that Keith had waited all these years to hear.

"You'll be fine, right, Daddy?" Abby asked, bringing him back to the moment.

"Of course I will, my girl. What about your wedding? Have you talked it over with Thomas? If there's any charge for changes or rearranging things, don't worry. I'll pick up the tab on that. Or Jay will. You know he'd do anything for you."

"The wedding is on, Dad. Same date. I spoke to Mom before she died, and she said she would want that. Bossy until the end!"

"That's your mom...That *was* your mom." Keith then added, "Abby...I'm glad you asked me to come and say goodbye to your mother. That was very sweet of you. It's just that I can't."

"You don't have to explain anything to me, Dad. I respect your decision."

He loved her clarity, her eloquence. It gave him the courage to offer her an apology.

"I know we seldom talk about your mom, but if you've ever doubted it, know that I loved your mother very, very much. I was a good husband to her. A really good husband. The few times you and I have spoken about the past, we've ended up angry, saying things we've both regretted. And I'm sorry for some of the things I've said about your mom."

"I know you were angry, Dad. Hurt."

"You were too young to understand. I never left her. I swear I didn't. I never left you and I never left your sisters. You and your sisters need to know that. It was your mother who walked out."

"Dad...I know all that. And so do Emma and Andrea. We know what happened. Aunt Rose told us her version over the years. We pieced together the whole truth. We knew then but we were too young to fully understand...Andrea and Emma understood better than I could. I was just too young. I've never doubted for one moment how much you loved my mom. I know you loved her fiercely. I know you never left her, and I never felt you left me in any way. Emma didn't either. Maybe Andrea did. Although deep down she knows you weren't to blame."

Chapter 12

Abby hesitated, and Keith heard the pause, the caution on the other end of the line. She continued, "What I've often wondered is whether you ever *stopped* loving her...I know you will always remember her, but this might be the right time to let go, Dad. Give yourself the chance to...let go..."

After her slow, broken words, it was Abby's turn to hear Keith's silence. She couldn't see her father, but she could imagine him trying to hold back his feelings, perhaps holding back tears.

Silence filled the hundreds of miles between father and daughter.

"I have to get back...Make arrangements..." Abby's voice trailed off.

"How many ways do I love thee?" Keith suddenly asked in their little childhood ritual. He had taught her that Elizabeth Barrett Browning sonnet when she was three years old and it had stayed with them forever. In spite of the slight misquote, they never thought of changing it.

"Let me count the ways," she replied as she always had.

"Love you, Abb!"

"Gotta go, Dad." And the phone went dead.

After she hung up, Keith could only think of his daughter and the deep pain she felt.

Then he thought of his own feelings, dull and brittle. He felt sad but almost relieved that Sam was finally gone. He suddenly felt able to breathe more easily.

He wanted to be there for his daughter as he had always attempted to be, but he also knew there are times that have to be faced alone. This was such a time for Abby. It would also give the three sisters a chance to spend time together, to console each other.

He knew they needed each other more than they cared to admit.

———————————◆◆◆◆◆◆◆◆◆◆◆———————————

Once again, Keith returned to the present, this warm day in July. He looked around, took a sip of his coffee, glanced at his watch, and realized that Jay was probably landing in Mexico City right about now.

Chapter 13

Keith walked a block south to the Zócalo, the very epicenter of the city, flagged a cab, and headed home. It was four-fifty in the afternoon.

As the cab hit traffic in the congested, bumpy avenues, Keith remembered his many encounters with Jay over the years. They had been so young and careless long ago, and so happy!

In spite of not attending the same school, in spite of hanging out with different crowds, they had remained friends to this day. Close friends.

After high school, Keith pursued a degree in art in California while Jay stayed in Mexico studying law.

Every summer, Keith came home to Mexico for a few weeks, dividing his stay between his parents' home and Jay's. With Jay's parents seldom home, they had a huge mansion and servants at their disposal, plenty of money to spend, and beautiful cars. It was heaven. They drank too much and chased women constantly.

Their only point of difference was cocaine: Keith never enjoyed it and couldn't get over the brutal aftermath, while Jay loved it, the up, the down, and the up again.

Years later, they both settled into the pursuit of their professions. Keith was a naturally gifted graphic designer working on retail design, logos, package design, and even set designs for major theatre productions. His practice grew along with his reputation, but financial gain was never his true motivation. He led a life of comfort, and Sam fell into that same comfort with ease once their relationship started. Only in time did she begin to miss the true wealth once a part of her previous marriage. This had been part of the peril of their relationship from day one and perhaps also her lifelong quest, sending her from relationship to relationship, wanting more, wanting to be richer, wanting whatever was next.

Jay spent the early years of his career as an attorney at a large international legal firm. When his parents died in an automobile crash, he was left with more money than he could ever need. Instead of sitting back and enjoying his wealth, his inner drive led him to start his own legal practice. In less than eight years, he had built one of the country's most well-recognized firms in a whirlwind run of smart legal maneuvering, uncanny business acumen, and diabolical energy. He redefined what working hard and playing hard truly meant. At age forty-one, he retired and started traveling the world with the spirit of a vagabond and the safety net of many millions tucked away in banks across the world.

Every few years, the two men's paths crossed, just as they would again in a few hours on this summer day.

In spite of their clear differences in attitudes and styles, they were always united by their belief in great ideas, albeit insane ones, and their love of gorgeous women.

Jay went through two wives before he was thirty, Keith serving as his best man, always a bit distant, a bit reluctant to commit so freely.

When Jay learned about Sam, he and Keith were sitting poolside at Jay's home in Mexico City. Jay vaguely recalled meeting her.

"I think I met her or her ex-husband some years ago. Alex Landa? Something like that?"

"That's his name. But you would remember her, Jay," Keith replied. "She's unbelievably beautiful."

"Miller, you say that about every woman you meet."

"Not like this, Jay. Norma was pretty, Alexandra was stunning, others were just good in bed, but Sam is amazing!"

"Which means only one thing; you're fucking her. Or, should I say, she's fucking the shit out of you. No wonder you've been smiling uncontrollably. You son of a bitch!"

"She might be the one."

"I've heard you say that before. Now one lives in Israel and the other one in Egypt. Is that a fucking coincidence or what? The two women you loved now live five thousand miles away from you in neighboring countries. They are neighbors, Egypt and Israel, right? I know they're close. Need I say more?"

"I really hadn't thought about that angle."

"Well, what are friends for if not to remind us of all the fuck-ups we've committed over the years and to encourage us to commit some more!"

"By the way, Sam's coming to Dallas with me. I took the job at Kramer and Pearlman."

"You're shitting me."

"No, I'm not. I accepted the offer two days ago: pretty good money, partner, hot assistant. Plus I have a couple of articles to write for a magazine on the side. Imagine that! How could I say no? Sam's going with me and I'm bringing her kids too. Two kids, gorgeous girls. One's nine and the little one is six now. You'll have to meet them."

"Meet them? Why would I do that?"

"For obvious reasons, you son of a bitch! You'll be their uncle now."

"No fucking way! Are you out of your mind? A woman with kids? Don't you want your own? Come on! Take the girl and fuck her all you want, but let the father take the kids. Jesus, Keith, you can't be serious!"

"You'll find yourself a new wife and have kids soon enough. It's my turn to settle down. Anyway, Samantha and I have talked it over. It's a done deal. We're going to Dallas in two weeks to look at houses."

"I don't know what to say."

"Shit, say what's on your mind. Isn't that what you always do? Or, for a change, you could say 'Congratulations, dear friend,' and mean it. It's pretty simple."

"You're a big boy, Keith. Hope it works out. I mean that. I hope you found *the* one. Congratulations. There, I said it."

"Wasn't that bad, was it?"

"We need to celebrate! When the fuck do I get to meet this angel, the future Mrs. Miller?"

"Mrs. Miller? Hold on! Who said anything about getting married?"

"I know you. You pretend to be liberal and a believer of free love, but all you want is a wedding with a bride in white, little flower girls, and all that shit! You'll be married within a year. You always want to preserve your image of decency, of old-fashioned charm. I'd bet you already have a place in mind. Anyway, you still have time before you really fuck up your life. Sleeping with one woman for the rest of your life," Jay mused. "One pussy for life. You are one weird fucker, my friend! So, when do I meet this person?"

"Tonight."

"Tonight?"

"What, are you busy, Jay? Big plans?"

"No. It just seems I'm being ambushed with all this information."

"Well?"

"I'm in, but are you sure? You know me. After the second bottle of wine, I'll tell her the truth about you. She might run. Or I might have to charm her and convince her that I'm the one she should run off into the sunset with."

"She's a decent woman. Not your type."

"Keith, they're all my type. The particular type just depends on the number of drinks. Plus women always prefer me over you as history has proven."

"Your number of drinks?"

"Theirs, of course! The drunker, the better. Then you can fuck them in the ass and they don't put up a fight!"

"You are fucking despicable...Please behave tonight."

"Don't I always?"

"Obviously not. If you did, we wouldn't be having this conversation."

"Where are you taking us?"

"You are taking us. That's proper etiquette!"

"Whatever, fucker."

"Cícero?" It was a favorite restaurant of theirs in downtown Mexico City where they'd had many an unforgettable night with friends and many, many women.

"Downtown? Will they still let us in?" Jay was referencing a night when he'd gotten into a heated debate with a group of people sitting at a nearby table that ended with broken noses, broken bottles, and broken chairs.

"When you pay, they let us in everywhere. Word of your generosity precedes you. Plus you apologized profusely to the owner that night."

"You should probably call so we get a table by one of the balconies."

"I already, did, my friend."

"Shit, you're such a *gringo*, Keith. Plan, plan, plan. Sometimes I wonder why you live in this country of beautiful chaos."

"That's exactly why I'll start my life with Sam away from here... And away from you!"

When Jay and Sam met that night, Keith was in heaven. The woman he loved and his best friend got along splendidly.

They went through five bottles of some obscenely priced wine that Jay ordered. When Keith got the bill he almost had a heart attack, but Jay stepped in, paying it gladly and gallantly as he always did in the presence of beautiful women.

The next morning, when Keith woke up, with Sam still asleep beside him, he called Jay.

Without any preamble, Jay told him, "She's a great girl, smoking hot. Only thing is, she's going to break your fucking heart. A woman like that has to be a bitch more often than not. She has that look in her eyes of a woman who will suck your dick dry, then chop it off without batting an eyelash. I'm sure that pussy is worth it, but it's gonna happen, man, and it's gonna hurt like hell...Just don't come crying to me and tell me I never warned you. Now go fuck your girlfriend and let me go back to sleep. Remember, there's nothing like a good fuck when you're severely hung over. It begins the healing. And Jay, don't ever call this fucking early again," and he promptly hung up.

Keith married Sam seven months later.

Jay himself married ten months later to the second of the three women to whom he said "I do."

Keith never fully understood how or why Jay knew Sam would break his heart. All he knew, years later, was that Jay had been right.

Chapter 14

There were so many things Keith was thankful for. In spite of his struggles, he had never let the disappointment of his relationship with Sam seep into his ability to be kind, to give of himself, to be amazed at the world.

After Abby left for college, he occasionally visited her old room and basked in the memories that lived and breathed in those four walls. As time would have it, Abby and her youth could not be disassociated from her mother, Samantha Riley. The more he tried to forget her, the more she inhabited his thoughts.

It was as if his love and need for Sam grew even as the force and constancy of those feelings propelled her in the opposite direction, away from him, losing definition and becoming ghostly memories of days he no longer knew or recognized as real.

He saw his years with Sam exactly for what they were: a truce, an interlude, *una tregua, mi tregua*. Everything before and everything after was the reality of his life, and a good reality in all fairness. Yet those years stood separate, a period of time with its own set of values and instances that had a unique finish, an afterglow, always a mystery, and now forever tainted with pain and betrayal.

Nonetheless, there were moments of great tenderness, of learning. Keith recognized unequivocally that the resentment of so many years toward Sam had eroded some of what he'd learned, but still his time with her had transformed his selfishness into a trait of giving that he was always thankful for.

With Sam, he'd learned to recognize and believe in the concept of *us*. Andrea and Emma and later Abby had taken his hand and, for a time, melted away the harshness, the cold, the angry shards of his being he'd always tried to keep in check.

With their innocent influence, he'd become someone who put others first. He was amazed by the fierceness of his protection toward Emma in particular. For a time, that child became his compass. He would have given his life for the charming little girl with eyes full of questions and peach fuzz on her cheeks.

Then Abby arrived just as Emma needed him less, or at least he believed, so his love poured out to his very own daughter for the rest of his life.

In the amazing hearts of his daughter and two stepdaughters, he learned to be a more gentle, more patient, more forgiving, and more giving version of himself.

He liked the man Sam and the girls helped him become and then left behind as they gradually left to follow their own paths, as wide in range as their personalities and outlooks on life.

Emma was the smartest. She had an ability to see the world and decipher it in an instant that moved her a million miles a minute to this and that and back again.

She also took to music as if Keith had poured it into her. They were so alike, sharing an impenetrable secret code that they themselves never understood, that both he and Sam found a faint, sad irony in the fact that Emma was not his daughter.

Andrea was a cat moving lazily yet gracefully through life and meadows. There were no words to describe the sweetness of those huge eyes that spoke such few words and yet said so much. At the same time, those eyes held enigmas that Keith could never decipher. God knows he'd tried.

Abby was a poet. From the moment she discovered words, she had decided to make her life with them. She was a happy girl with a streak of sadness that showed itself at times in the shadows of her wonderful liquid brown eyes. It was a sadness that came from another life, from another century, as if Abby had lived a hundred lives earlier and was still searching for something she could not quite identify but knew she needed.

Sam had opened a window into a world Keith had never imagined in all its colors and expansiveness. With her, he learned to live a life he'd only read about in books and seen in the glossy photographs of magazines. A life filled with laughter, kids, SUVs, and extracurricular activities.

He watched for years as the girls explored dance classes, soccer, baseball, painting. He instilled in them a love of violins, flutes, and the countless guitars that filled his small studio.

The memories of those days, of the breathtaking moments of seeing his girls score a goal or sing at a recital or be chosen to carry the flag at school, reminded him that he had much to be grateful for.

Without Samantha, those memories would never have been his. Samantha, that uncanny mix of mother hen and vixen that made her inherently attractive and dangerous all in an instant, in a single batting of the eyelashes. She was made from earth and silk, both so distinct and yet so curiously connected in their origin.

But there was a hard surface that shined and occasionally showed more surface beneath it, as if substance weren't needed.

His thoughts always concluded by wondering what Sam might remember, what deeply held treasure she might keep somewhere in her heart. Had she ever kept a longing for his love? Had she ever wondered if his door had remained open? Had she ever run to his side but found him away, traveling somewhere? Had she left a note that a strong wind had swept into nothingness?

Alas, Keith knew the answer. Inexplicably, she had not.

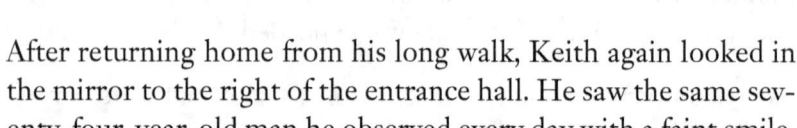

After returning home from his long walk, Keith again looked in the mirror to the right of the entrance hall. He saw the same seventy-four-year-old man he observed every day with a faint smile, brown eyes, and a few remaining strands of hair locked firmly in place by extra-hold hair gel.

It was July 10 in Cuernavaca, and the wait for his friend was over.

He heard a car pull into the driveway and the bell at the gate ring. He turned to the clock in the kitchen and saw that it was exactly six-seventeen in the evening. The sun was close to setting, and a slight, fresh breeze swept through the lush yard.

Keith still had the same maid his mother had employed for forty-five years. Rosa had started coming to his mother's house when she was thirteen and was now a great grandmother twice over.

"*Yo creo que ya llegó el Señor Jay,*" she said as she slowly stood up from the small bench in the kitchen where she had eaten her meals for more than forty years.

"I'll get the door, Rosa," Keith said. "Why don't you get out some glasses instead?"

Although Rosa was younger than Keith, he had noticed the vicious swelling of her legs and how she struggled to move. Maybe it was time for her to retire. Perhaps one of her great granddaughters could come in her place.

Keith chuckled at the thought. He prided himself on being a gentleman, but perhaps it wasn't a good idea to have a hard-bodied seventeen-year-old with skin the color of chocolate milk running around the house, especially with Jay visiting.

Jay was already opening the wrought iron gate. He had brought a small roller bag and a backpack and was wearing a long black gabardine that Keith suspected was the same one he'd worn that late November day in New York when they'd last bumped into each other.

Keith had been coming out of the New York Palace, a hotel he stayed at frequently. It was dusk and freezing outside as he pushed through the revolving door leading onto 50th Street, feeling the heater above for a moment before being hit by the wind as it swayed audibly through the streets. Late November in New York was beautiful. Today it was also cold.

The men wore heavy overcoats and dark shoes but the women knew better. They wore vests and coats and furs and hats. Young and old, they were bundles of beauty and purpose as they marched with laptops, briefcases, purses, clutches, and shopping bags. Some scowled, some prayed, some smiled openly, and some smiled only to themselves.

They were everywhere, in the streets, in the restaurants, and in grills and bistros. They were window shopping alone and linked arm in arm as they crossed the cold, congested streets. They were in the reflections of the stunningly decorated windows of the shops that lined Madison and 5th Avenue and every street in between. They were also reflected in the puddles left behind by the passing rain. They hailed cabs, descended from town cars and buses, and emerged from the mouths of darkened subway stations. Occasionally they flirted with passing men who smiled, fleetingly touched by these angels who played with their hair and scarves just as they played with their children.

Women were everywhere, and Keith loved women.

As soon as he stepped out from the hotel, he saw Jay walking in.

Typical Jay. Wearing that black raincoat with a black scarf, cigarette in hand, looking as if he hadn't slept in a year or two. The attorney with Canali suits had called it quits, retiring young, smoking incessantly, scoring good cocaine when he fancied it, and drinking as if the end of the world were near. On the edge, all or nothing. The two friends couldn't have been more different.

"All these years, I've been led to believe this is one of the nicest hotels in the city, but if they're letting you stay here, the standards have either been lowered or these are tough times for the lodging industry."

At the sound of his friend's voice, Jay turned. "Keith! Keith! Or at least what's left of my dear old friend!"

They hugged and kissed and Jay introduced the gorgeous young woman standing next to him, also smoking and rocking side to side to keep warm.

"Mother of God, Matilda!" Before him stood one of the most beautiful women Keith had ever seen. "I saw you when you were seven, and look at you now!"

"*Qué tal Keith*?" she said in the most friendly of greetings with an accent that Keith failed to place, half Spain, half Brit.

He knew Jay had a daughter from his second marriage, but after that divorce and two additional marriages plus countless other love interests, Keith had lost track of the girl and her mother.

Jay saw Keith caught off guard by the stunning beauty before him.

"You're going to pop an artery, Miller. Enough with the staring, old fucker. I catch you looking at my daughter's ass, who happens to turn twenty-two in a week, and I will fucking kill you. *Estamos?*"

The three of them laughed, huddling together to avoid yet another gust of wind that whistled by them, billowing their coats and Matilda's hair.

"Ay, Papá, que el tío Keith está casi tan bien como cuando eran jóvenes," she smiled at both men.

Even as he heard the harsh Spanish accent that came from the girl's mother and saw the beauty of Jay's second wife, Camila, a stunning model who had ditched Jay for a hot young Spanish actor, Keith felt flattered. Matilda had said, "Oh, Dad, this man is looking as good as he did when both of you were young."

He recalled Jay saying once with poignant humor, "Keith, every man should love a whore once in his life. And every man should love a goddess once in his lifetime. The problem is knowing which one is which. I had Camila; you had Samantha. Were they whores or goddesses? Only you and I know the answer. Or so we think. And it really doesn't matter because we are destined to be wrong."

"So, what brings you here? Don't tell me you're living here," Keith asked, but Matilda quickly answered.

"I've just transferred to NYU. And my father, contrary to what most people think, has recently discovered some fatherly protective instinct toward me that is simply moving," and she smiled at both of the old men who walked beside her.

"So, Keith, what brings you to New York? Work, I suppose?"

"Some work, some play."

"We were just about to change and then head out to dinner, so case closed: you're coming with us."

"I'm in."

And off they went.

The evening ended like the countless nights before it: very late, or very early, depending on your perspective, with memories demystified and rearranged, with laughter that didn't end, and a bill at the restaurant that simply could not be possible.

When they arrived at the hotel lobby, Matilda excused herself and Jay and Keith sat at the bar to have *la última*, the last drink of the night. The bartender, who was about to close, rolled his eyes but poured them a last drink.

"Remember that girl you almost fucked in Austin all those years ago?" Jay began good-naturedly.

"That came out of left field. But as a matter of fact, I do. Her name was Melissa. What was I thinking? And what's with the question now?"

"You should've fucked her. It was your preemptive strike against Sam."

"You never know," Keith replied, evading the comment and where it might lead.

"That woman should have kicked the shit out of you. Or some-one should have. Gorgeous woman, and you got all Southern Baptist on her. Fuck you, Miller. A girl wants to get fucked, who are you to deny her that unalienable right. Jesus, it's in the Constitution."

"Well, I kept thinking of Sam."

"Sam? Dear God, you were so fucking lost. What did that woman ever give you? Face the facts, Keith. She dumped you the minute she found what she wanted: more money, nothing more and nothing less. And a green card. Let's not forget the green cards for her and her children. All she wanted from you was money and her residency card in the US. You followed your dick and fell right into her trap. Years after, several more marriages later, she's still fucking someone for money. Even in that she fucked up... well, at least you have Abby."

"What's that supposed to mean, Jay?"

"What?"

"'At least you have Abby.'"

"Shit, my friend. Exactly that: You have Abby. The best thing that came from your pseudo-marriage to that cunt."

"Watch it, Jay. You have no right to call Sam that." Keith's voice turned to ice.

"*Cunt?* Are we getting sensitive in our middle age, Keith?"

"Let's just drop the *cunt* thing. I know you never thought much of Sam and always warned me not to fall for her, but c'mon; she's Abby's mother."

"First of all, my chivalrous friend, you don't tell me what to say. Second, you're the one who brings her up in every conversation. Like an hour ago. So get the fuck over it. It's about time, Keith. Stop feeling sorry for yourself. We all lose someone we love. It's life and it can be a bitch, but you move on."

"Unlike you, Jay, I actually care about other human beings."

"Ooh, my! It seems somebody's a bit sensitive today."

"Fuck you."

"See you around when you're not having your period, Keith. Just don't forget the bill. It's your turn for once. And please don't start crying in your drink."

Jay finished his drink, stood up, and walked out without looking at his friend.

Keith sat alone for a few minutes as the lobby activity died and the lights dimmed. He knew there was truth in Jay's words, but still they stung. He also knew that all these words would be forgotten in the morning.

As he waited for the bill to arrive, he thought back to the earlier part of the evening. Matilda, following in her father's steps, was a stunning, raging alcoholic in the making and a wonderful storyteller. She was full of the youth that Jay, Keith, and Sam had shared long ago.

What surprised him most was the look of pride he'd seen in Jay's eyes when he gazed at his daughter. So there was a heart somewhere in that son of a bitch after all, Keith mused as he staggered to his room.

He saw that look again as they regrouped for a late breakfast the next morning. Of course, no mention was made of the harsh words spoken between the two men the night before. All was forgiven, as it always had been.

＊◆＊◆＊◆＊◆＊◆＊

Jay brought a breath of fresh air to the world of order and caution in which Keith enclosed himself.

They embraced, these two old men who had seen so much life, who had spent so many days on their own, who had seen so much of life together: the most wonderful moments and the toughest of times.

Rosa was waiting at the door when Jay and Keith walked into the house. Jay had known her for years, had seen her age. He hugged her, catching her off guard, creating an awkward moment for her since it breached the lines between classes that still remained in Mexico. But, of course, Jay didn't abide by such lines nor did he care about them.

"*Doña Rosa, qué gusto verla.*"

Rosa set glasses on the terrace along with an unopened bottle of fine tequila, one of several Keith had bought in preparation for Jay's visit.

"Keith! Your house continues to be so fucking neat it makes me uncomfortable. I'm afraid I might break something. Let me start moving things. Might as well get used to me." Jay set his bag down and sat on the long wicker couch where he'd reclined a thousand times before.

In spite of his dear friend's relentless sense of order, Jay still recognized the beauty of Keith's arrangements. Every picture was arranged with a keen eye for design. The flowers on the tables were casually set with the hand of an intuitive and innate art director, while the garden was an intricate mosaic of color and textures years in the making.

That garden was in full bloom, and Jay realized the miracle of plants and flowers in these latitudes. Everything grew and blossomed with ease and certainty, never fearing the droughts, snow, or ice of more northern places.

Jay looked at the photos on the side tables. He saw himself in a few of them, some of them taken with Keith back when they both had lots of hair and looked gallantly into the camera, so vital, so fucking sure of themselves. He saw photos of Keith's parents. He saw the picture he'd seen a thousand times of himself with Keith's daughter Abby and his step-daughters Andrea and Emma.

The three girls loved jumping on Jay and visiting his home, a whole different universe for them.

At Jay's, they could yell and jump on the couches and use their crayons and markers on the wooden table in Jay's study. When Keith first started taking the girls to visit his friend, they were cautious and respectful, but Jay gave them scissors and access to the hundreds of pens and markers with which he pursued his love of painting, drawing, and senseless ideation after retirement.

The girls immediately found huge pieces of paper to draw on until Jay took it away and invited them to draw on the wooden table itself. At first, the girls were hesitant, but they soon found the courage and freedom to explore the feel of those markers, leaving their designs and childhood drawings forever seeped into the dry wood.

They loved Jay as the kind friend of their father who let them do things they would never dream of trying in their father's home.

As Jay continued a slow inspection of the framed photographs, each one seemed to come alive, eager to tell its own story.

Some were simple pictures taken at a moment's whim. Jay glanced at the photograph of Keith and his brother Tony with their parents by a Christmas tree. At Abby and Keith's mom sitting in a hammock, smiling as Abby read to her grandmother. At a photo of Jay and Keith as teenagers, gangly and unsure of themselves but still challenging the world with their will and youthful arrogance.

Other photographs marked special events. There was one of Abby at her first ballet recital, standing proudly at age seven. Keith and Tony somewhere in their teens, long-haired, trying to look like rock stars. Abby at her wedding, dressed in white and looking as beautiful as the dreams of her youth. A sepia portrait of Keith's parents on their wedding day, showing a young woman and a young man happy and bewildered by the moment, by the uncertainty of the voyage they were about to embark on.

Jay walked once more around the living room and then stepped outside as the sunset became centered in the window. Keith joined him, opening the bottle reserved for the occasion and pouring carefully into the small glasses before them. He filled them to the brim, and they raised their glasses in the toast that had started with Gatorade as kids, then moved to a few beers as teens and then to good liquor when they could afford it.

They sat for hours, laughing endlessly at the adventures that life had let them experience. Their glasses were filled again and again without worries, without concern, without guilt. Jay told stories that made no sense while Keith told stories that made too much sense.

Although they felt full of life, with many stories yet to write and retell in evenings just like this, any passerby would have seen two old men huddled together with a thousand wrinkles that spoke of lives lived well, with purpose and with the inquisitiveness that took them to distant lands and to worlds that at times had spun out of control.

They had loved every minute of it.

The passerby would have been touched by the eyes of both men that shined as they remembered the days of their youth, their friends, the women they had loved, the children they were leaving in this world, convinced it was a better world simply because their children were in it.

"It's good to see you, Jay," Keith said, and Jay responded with the *joie-de-vivre* that refused to die.

"Now don't start getting all emotional on me, you old fuck! We're going to have a great time."

"How long are you planning to stay?"

"Why start with questions you know damn well I have no answer to? Are you trying to get rid of me already? I got here an hour ago. At least wait until tomorrow for that."

"I have no idea why I asked that. I should know better. So, where have you been these last few months?"

"Here. There. And back again."

As they spoke about their latest ins and outs, they eventually discussed their daughters. They agreed, as they rarely did, that having a daughter was a blessing. It was strange that, after all the years, Abby and Matilda had never met.

"Who knows, they'll probably meet when one of us dies," one of them said.

"That is fucking depressing, but likely true."

"We should take a trip with them. Somewhere. Your treat, you fucking miser," Keith suggested. "Still have tons of money stashed away in a Swiss bank?"

"There's still some left, enough for Matilda and that lazy husband of hers to live very well for years to come. You met him. You were at their wedding, right?"

"I was."

"How are you doing on money? Need some? You know you can always count on me." Jay took a long sip of his drink.

"I'm fine, Jay. These days my needs are simple. I go out very little. I only spend money when I visit Abby. But how about taking the girls on a trip?"

"Keith, Matilda and Abigail are grown women now. They don't want to be seen with us anywhere in the world. Besides, I'm not taking two middle-aged women, their husbands, and some snotty little kids on a cruise. Forget it, my friend. Give the girls a break. Shit! Give us a break. All they want is for us to die, preferably peacefully and soon so they can sell our homes, get rid of all our shit, and run off with the money!"

Both men laughed.

Jay then narrated some of the highlights of his last couple of years and specific escapades in New York, Rome, Santo Domingo, and Panama.

"Rome, Santo Domingo, and New York, I can see the attraction, but Panama?" Keith asked. "Never been there. Have you developed an interest in maritime engineering I should know about? Do you have yet another wife hidden down there?"

"Hell no. Wife? Are you fucking kidding me? They just happen to have good rum and cheap hookers, or cheap rum and good hookers. I can't remember which. Before I forget, by the way, happy birthday, old man."

"Thanks. I'm surprised you still remember."

"I am more surprised *you* remember."

"I'm not the one who's been frying his brain for sixty years. At least not that much. I also remember that yours will be what? Two days from today? Sunday?"

"That's about right. By the way, I brought some superb hash from Morocco."

"Jesus, Jay! Do you know the risk you took? You really want to end your days in a Mexican jail? Holy shit! You might be an old man, but some punk is still gonna want to fuck you *por el culo*, my dear," Keith told him and laughed loudly, loosely.

"Relax, old man. Do you think they would imagine this distinguished-looking gentleman is carrying a nice little stash?"

"You still act as if you were fifteen! In reality, you're an old man in his midseventies."

"Thank God. I'd rather act fifteen than a hundred and twenty, like you do, you grumpy old fucker."

"Grumpy, my ass. I am very happy...By the way, Abby called this morning to wish me a happy birthday and I told her you were arriving. She said to say hi and sends her love."

"Send her my love right back. That is one fabulous kid. You did okay, Keith. After all these years, I have to tell you that I regret not spending more time with Matilda when she was young. I always thought there would be time for that."

"We just thought differently about our role as fathers. Nothing wrong with that, right?"

"It's a bit more complicated than that. I allowed myself to miss being there for her. It's funny because I don't regret missing birthdays or recitals. It's the simple, everyday things like when she said her first word or the day she fell off her Ripstick or whatever those things are called. I missed knowing who her first boyfriend was and when she had her first kiss. She's never shared those things. I have few memories of her as a little kid."

"It's never too late to be a better father, to make those memories, Jay. They are made diligently, every day, by being there. That's all it takes. You know that, don't you?"

"It's just that *being there*, as you say, is not my thing. I've always been good at going places, not at being *in* places. And I'm not sure kids can forgive that easily."

"Matilda has nothing to forgive you for. You were the best father you knew how to be. I was the best father I knew how to be. We made mistakes and we scored some hits. Our kids turned out all right. It's funny, thinking of our daughters as kids," Keith added. "They're both in their midforties or somewhere around there."

"They're fast catching up with us."

"So, what are we going to do these next few days?" Keith asked, already red from consuming half the bottle of tequila.

Jay stood up and patted his friend on the back. "Well, what have we been doing for the past sixty-some years, my friend? We'll find some pretty women and get us some pussy!"

They laughed out loud as their glasses clinked again in the toast of a thousand nights before, their eyes crinkling in joy at the years shared and the days ahead.

Sometimes it seemed like they had closed their eyes for just a moment after that first tennis match some half dozen decades before. Even if they had known then where life would take them, they never would have believed the journey.

Looking out at the night, Keith saw a single star, the first one on the horizon. For the briefest of moments, just as he had countless nights before, he thought that Sam would have loved tonight's sky.

Chapter 15

The pause outside the Chinese restaurant where Keith and Samantha kissed freely for the first time stayed with him forever, soaking in the river through which their story flowed.

It was an odd place to stop and kiss, amongst the roaring bustle of the big city, but passion overcame them there as love grew inside them.

That day, their kisses were a promise made in the warm, hazy afternoon. Perhaps it was because the city was set so high in the valley between the high plains of their heart's country that they felt they could touch the sky. And that simple fact was left behind in their memories.

The peaceful, easy conversation they shared sitting on the hardwood floor of the gym that Sam had once owned remained an equally peaceful, easy memory. That conversation had led to a dance, slow and steady, as love pushed them closer and closer. The songs were forgotten, perhaps old Luis Miguel *boleros*, but the closeness, the warmth, never would be.

The memory of the weight of Sam's leg over Keith as they slept kept coming back, as if its very absence amplified and served as a metaphor for the void, the weightlessness, the lack of purpose of his days after she left.

Raw urgency crisscrossed his senses in the afterlife, just as it had the nights they'd made love in a state that was half asleep and half awake. Keith came closer to Sam, almost by a fortuitous movement, and she just as fortuitously wrapped her arms and legs around him, bringing him not only into her body but into her dreams as well. And when sleep overcame them, they continued to dream that they lived in each other's dream.

Hatred toward Sam along with her many fuck-buddies, those before and those after, who came and went with the years, haunted Keith. Horrific imagery took hold at times, and only the thought of Abby could evaporate it, for she instantly made him a better man, one capable of forgiveness. Yet in spite of her, a rage he never knew he could hold in his soul became the faithful companion to his memories of Sam. Together, the memories, rage, and solitude kept each other company in Keith's heart throughout the cold of real and imaginary winters. And as much hatred as he felt for Sam at times for her betrayal, it never came close to his own self-hatred for allowing her to take advantage of his love and trust for so long.

He recalled the evening Sam had reached for his hand and taken it to her middle. Keith was half asleep and didn't understand until he felt the movement, the kick. "That's our daughter, Keith," she had said. She didn't have to say anything more. Keith understood. Emotion grew as he realized that moving being inside his wife would alter his life forever. He had waited for this moment a lifetime. He fell asleep with his hand on Sam's stomach, waiting for another movement, wanting this moment to last and last.

An afternoon in the park on a cold afternoon around Thanksgiving was one of his treasures. Sam was there, Andrea was there, and

Emma was there. Abby had not been born yet. Keith felt as if God had given him so much in these three women, and he wasn't sure why. What had he done to deserve these three princesses with their hair dancing in the wind, the three of them pushing it behind their left ears, almost at the same time, in a movement that seemed perfectly choreographed.

He recalled another afternoon when, in the middle of a main avenue in Mexico City, Sam got out of a friend's car and ran to Keith's. Keith heard honking and whistles as she raced barefoot to the passenger door, high heels dangling from her hand, looking so beautifully out of place in the middle of the congested intersection.

He remembered a snowy New Year's Day when they'd awakened late and Sam had opened the curtains and asked Keith to come see. He recalled walking half asleep to the window and taking Sam in his arms. They'd stayed for a few minutes holding each other, looking out the window, as the snow fell over Paris. Keith remembered thinking that life could not give them anything more as the snow continued to fall and the three girls slept in heavenly peace in the adjoining room in the small hotel more than four thousand miles from home. Home then was not a specific geography or a well-defined latitude but the simple time and place where they held each other.

Then there was their last vacation together when the girls were still young and all five of them walked on the soft beach, sharing a horizon that gave them a sense of solidarity and closeness. Little did he know that dark clouds were soon to follow and that moment would be the last time they would all hold hands. Never more would all five smiles shine together in a photograph that would peel with time as their skin had that long-ago summer after turning dark brown from the sun.

Sam took his hand in hers one day. She simply reached over as she drove and took his hand. He felt as if they would be forever bonded by this, the most simple, human, and ancestral gesture of a woman's hand in a man's hand, a sign of unity, of mutual belonging. In that instant, Keith knew he would love Samantha a lifetime and that she'd leave an imprint of such significance that it would remain with him the rest of his life. With their hands united, he knew he was as close to heaven as he'd ever be. If ever Keith knew happiness, it was in the ethereal memories of simple moments, simple acts, simple words. Happiness seemed to exist in the trivial, everyday ribbons of unexpectedness.

Each of these moments remained engraved in a memory that was part of several lives. And maybe that was what defined a family, Keith reflected, that shared pool of memories from which all participants partake. Sure, time had softened the etchings, but after half a lifetime, the memories stayed, elusive and translucent, suspended in time.

———————◆◆◆◆◆◆◆◆———————

Fumbling in the darkness, Keith reached for a glass of water. The afternoon with Jay had turned to late evening. Lots of tequila had been drunk until the two old men said their last *salud*.

It had been a good day, this July 10. Keith dropped his clothes in a pile by the bed. He felt heavy and drowsy from too many drinks but happy nonetheless. He and Jay had laughed and reminisced as he'd known they would. They'd argued and reassembled memories. That's what friends were for: to keep you company so that the journey, at least sometimes, has a purpose.

Then he turned out the light and fell into a dreamless, restless sleep.

Chapter 16

Keith sat in the back of the car for more than an hour, gazing intently at the surroundings as the city gave way to green meadows covered in white snow that continued to fall.

He'd given the driver the directions the hotel had printed for him. It was a bitterly cold day in February, and the falling snow made it hard to follow the road.

He loved this city. He hadn't been back in more than twenty years, and he knew this might be the last time he'd visit this side of the ocean.

He had debated taking this trip for a long time. With vestiges of long-worn bitterness, he admitted to himself that coming here was a lack of commitment to his own promise to never visit Sam's final resting place.

Then he'd realized that, since he was about to turn eighty and had reached what would probably be the last few years of his life, he really didn't care. He had earned the right to do whatever he wanted. He wanted to come and say good-bye, and he wanted to do it alone. He hadn't even told Abby he was coming.

He finally reached the gates of the cemetery. It had taken him more than seventeen years to visit, but he was an old man now, and he wanted his last trip to have special meaning.

Thus, London was his destination.

He asked the driver to park the car and wait for him. It was bitterly cold. He walked to the cemetery office and gave Sam's name to a sweet elderly woman who looked in some huge brown binders and gave him instructions on where the grave was located.

As he was walking back toward the door, in a proper British accent, the woman sweetly asked, "Did you know her? Are you a family member?"

He turned and smiled ruefully. "I did know her. And, yes, she was once family."

"You must have loved her indeed to come out on a day like this." The woman spoke with an earnestness that made Keith smile.

"It was long ago. It's hard to remember those days."

"Well, we still know those things. I do, indeed," she replied with conviction.

"Sometimes too much time has passed for us to remember."

"I tell people who come that their loved one resting here knows when someone visits. I do," she concluded emphatically.

"I hope you're right...Have a good day, ma'am."

"Cover up. It's starting to snow again," she replied pleasantly.

Keith stepped out into the cold and walked among the rows of small stone markers carrying nothing but the simple white carnations he'd brought.

To the surprise of her daughters, her latest husband, and her friends, Sam had left precise instructions to be buried next to her parents in England. She had arranged everything and had paid for a small plot to the right of her mother and father in this cemetery in the outskirts of London.

Keith walked until he reached the top of a small hill overlooking a beautiful pond and found Sam's headstone. He was surprised to see that it was engraved with her name, the years of her birth and death, and nothing more. He felt this was a contradiction to the life she had lived, a life defined by killer looks, of form above substance, a life in which even love had to look great and be embodied in a jewel or fine dress.

It seemed odd that she would choose to lie here in a place so far from the sunshine and hometown that had adopted her, so far from her world, so far from her children.

Perhaps she wanted a proximity to her parents that she had never had in life, a return to where her journey had started.

At the same time, her choice of burial location revealed that unexpected free spirit that had taken her to so many places and experiences. Perhaps, in the years before her death, Sam had finally found who she was and where she belonged.

Keith clung to the concept that, as far removed as they were, as much distance as they had placed between them, they were still the two travelers they had always been, crossing paths through life.

In spite of the miles separating them, he was convinced they had both stood in awe at the same expanse of sky, had both felt small and insignificant amidst the countless stars, had both admired the same moon at the exact same moment.

He was sure they had stood on opposite shores of the same ocean, he on his coast and Sam on hers, admiring the perfect curvature of the Earth and wondering if there was someone standing on the other side, feeling the same breeze, wetting their feet in the same ocean.

He felt this was a perfect metaphor for the striking differences that had attracted them initially and then sent them careening into their other spaces, their other selves, their other lives.

Keith stood by Sam's grave and prayed to God for forgiveness for all the times he had shouted her name in rage, for every shred of hatred that had come to live in his heart, making him blame her for the many years of solitude that were as bitter as the cold of this afternoon, thousands of miles away from the town where the sun had blessed them.

He also thanked God for giving him the chance to find the woman he had once believed to be his soul mate, the woman who was the mother of his child. He thanked God for having placed them on that playground decades earlier, where they'd innocently smiled at one another.

In spite of how it had ended, Sam was the woman who had taught him to love with no boundaries, with the simple unwavering conviction that she had been sent to him from the very beginning of time, as if the centuries had merely been a preparation for her arrival.

The days he had spent with her were some of the most wonderful days of his life. Her happiness had fed his, and it no longer mattered what those days might have meant to Sam.

If they had been only a simple refuge, a moment to catch her breath before setting off once again on her journey, Keith hoped she had felt his love and that she had been left with some joy, some comfort, some certainty of having being loved honestly and fiercely.

Keith took out a brief poem written many years earlier by a poet who could put into words the things Keith sensed but felt incapable of articulating.

He had typed it neatly in small letters on a pristine piece of paper. He took it from his coat, unfolded it, and read fragments slowly against the cold wind.

...only then did he think of her,
choosing her
and without pain
without desperations
without anguish
and without fear
without objection
he began
as in other nights before
to need her.

* Mario Benedetti (La Otra Copa Del Brindis)

•••••••••

Keith read the words out loud to Sam, his Sam, to his fading memory of the Sam of long ago.

He read the lines slowly to the cold wind around him, hoping they would reach her in that place far away where perhaps she had finally found peace. He could feel her presence in the myriad of memories tattooed on his soul and skin, and although she had passed long ago, Keith knew she would live within him forever.

There were times when he simply let himself be washed in a soft light that he knew was Sam. It had no physical quality; it was not her features or her body or her laughter but rather her spirit that visited him, a faint breeze that passed by every now and then.

He saw her vividly now, walking toward him with that perfect smile, that dancing laughter, the wondrous stories she told and that he believed to this day. He knew she was there. Close.

At the same time, he knew that visiting her here would allow him to finally abandon her, would set him free. The invisible presence of so many years, inhabiting him silently, would vanish.

He spoke slowly. "You have lived forever in my heart, Samantha Riley. And today I came to say good-bye."

The memories that came to life were as real as her remains resting in the ground, but the weight that had oppressed him for so long finally lifted.

As he had once before, Keith swore he'd keep his promise to her as he placed the flowers on the ground and kissed the cold stone.

He suddenly realized that, once again, they were sharing this exact moment in time, on this precise patch of cold grass, looking out to the same horizon, as he had dreamt on countless nights that they would one day do again.

One more day together was all he had asked for, and today his wish was being granted.

Separated by only a crust of dirt, it didn't matter who lived and who didn't. All that mattered was that they were again traveling together, that boy and that girl, speeding on this Earth as forces beyond their comprehension propelled them through this vast and wonderful universe to new endings and new beginnings.

Keith turned and began walking up the slight slope. He stopped once, briefly, knowing he'd never return, knowing he'd done the right thing in coming. He had said farewell.

As he departed, the wind picked up, scattering leaves in a beautiful swirl of brown and red that contrasted with the pure white snow falling about him.

Chapter 16

The sudden wind quieted, the leaves falling silently and lightly to the ground, as Keith reached the top of the hill. He held his overcoat tightly to his neck, seeking a bit of warmth. Although he knew he'd never return to this place outside of London, he never looked back.

The hour-long ride to the city was silent as the driver took him closer and closer to London's center. In the car, in the dwindling light of the cold afternoon, Keith felt as if a large weight had been lifted from his shoulders.

Yes, he thought of Sam. After all, he'd come because of her. But he felt as if he could place her outside of him now, see her more objectively, recognize the once familiar warmth, her laughter, the beautiful features of her youth, but also now look into her darkness, her genuine lack of depth, her selfishness, her fading beauty.

The torrential flow of emotions that had coursed through him for years dissipated. There was peace, an opaqueness to the memories, that placed them in their true meaning and context. From this perspective, the feelings were soft and comfortable, as if the edges that occasionally shone and cut through had disintegrated and blown into the fog that surrounded him as he exited the car in front of the hotel.

As Keith walked up the steps to the lobby, he turned to see the car depart in the mist of the early evening and smiled to himself. He was starting a new time, a new path. Where it would take him, nobody knew, but he was eager to see where it might lead.

The After

It was evening when Abby opened her forever box. She was now eighty-four years old. Her two grown-up sons, Tommy and Sebastian, were in their fifties, and both lived far away. She was a grandmother to three young men and one beautiful grand-daughter. She was also a great-grandmother to a delightful pair of twins.

Thomas and one or two men who had shared her path after she was widowed were gone now, too. A few friends remained, too frail to visit, but she loved her solitude. She read and watched movies voraciously. She moved slowly these days.

She looked out her window in the growing dusk and saw the gray clouds and falling rain. It was always on days like this that she brought the box down and saw her story, her life, and relived the memories that time often fades. Some memories were thin and uncertain, but others remained well defined and vivid.

She had lived a great life. She had married a man who adored her and stayed with her until he passed away. As the child of divorce, she had fought hard to nurture her marriage. They'd experienced a few tough times, as couples do, but she and Thomas had always found renewed respect and a tenderness that kept them close. They had both worked hard to attain the material comfort and success that perhaps her father had not adequately provided her mother. While they had lived well, Abby mused, her mother had always wanted something more, something better, although Abby remained unsure of what exactly that might have been.

She and Thomas had traveled extensively. They had provided Tommy and Sebastian with the luxuries that hard work allows, and the boys had attended the best schools and universities. Years later, she had sold the small brownstone they had toiled hard to buy after they moved to New York, and had bought a small cottage on the North Carolina coast. It was a simple life, wanting nothing, and with few regrets.

Abby wished her mother had lived to see her grandchildren grow up. Abby had great memories of her own grandparents, particularly her father's mom. When Abby was very young and had lived with her dad, Marisa had come to live with them to help raise her granddaughter. Her father had always found it odd and endearing that his seventy-year-old mother and young toddler enjoyed each other's company so much.

Abby was sorry her own sons didn't have that closeness with her parents. Her father had visited occasionally and the boys had adored him, but it was her mother that Abby herself missed most. She missed hearing her stories and having her as a friend, someone to confide in during her adult life. As much as she adored her father and acknowledged his role in her life, there were things she could never talk to him about.

Abby peered into the box in front of her. She touched the fabric of her school uniform that her father had saved inside a plastic bag. God knew why! She looked at the fading photographs of her sisters and herself, all three smiling. Andrea almost a young woman of fourteen; Emma at twelve or eleven, looking as if she were up to no good; Abby at four, hugging her sisters. There was a photo of her mom in a black-and-white portrait, looking like a movie star, almost regal in her beauty.

There was a blanket, or what was left of it, frayed and faded. Abby could still imagine her mother knitting it. She recalled waiting impatiently by the laundry room whenever it found its way into the gentle cycle of the washer.

There were drawings, birthday cards, and faded programs from plays and concerts she and her father had enjoyed. There was her first boarding pass from when she was just two months old. There were a few small dolls and a jewelry box with her engagement ring from Thomas, a gold Rolex her mother had left her, the earrings her father had bought her long ago when she was still a young girl. There were a few other things she had not passed on to her sons and their wives that she was saving for her only granddaughter, little Samantha. Her mother had never met her namesake, having passed away years before she was born, but the resemblance between them was eerie.

There were hundreds of other photographs, mainly of Abby and her father, a lifetime that her father had diligently recorded so there would always be a testament to their story.

Toward the bottom, she found what she was looking for.

For the hundredth time, she found the brief note her father had written for her mother so many years before. She wished her mother had read it, if only once, but Abby knew she never had because she had found it among her mother's belongings in an unopened envelope. It was dated twenty years after her parents had separated, not long before her mother passed. Her father had said that one day he would find a way to speak again to her mother. Abby had assumed he wanted to give her words of kindness that neither of them had afforded the other in life.

She preferred not to dwell on the bitterness she had felt pass between them so often. Instead, she rearranged memories and conversations so that she could find the signs of love that had once existed. When she found the letter after her mother passed away, she read it once and threw it out. It was a letter from her father to her mother, and they, or rather *he*, deserved his dignity and his privacy. It said what Abby knew her father had kept inside him for almost forty years.

Inside the letter, there had also been a brief note, a poem of sorts. Abby had kept that. It gave her a sense of belonging that had sometimes eluded her throughout life. She convinced herself that, as the daughter of this man and this woman whose paths had crossed not once but twice, she had a right to know about them and the right to keep the last thread that connected them to each other.

And so, she read the poem again:

The Kiss of That Boy & That Girl

To Sam

Their kiss was the condensed history of kissing. It went from tracing over that first touching kiss of twenty some years ago when they had been just children to the probing exercise of the girl and the boy twenty-some years later, now grown up and wanting more, kissing with urgency, wanting to drink each other.

Their kiss was the coming together of their lips in the manner of forever. It was the search for the perfect congruency of his mouth on hers. Hers on his. It was the tentative opening of lips, allowing more of the other to come into the other.

This kiss, always to be cherished, was the kiss of rain in the afternoon of any given day, where rain became the river that washed away other times and other stories and, of course, the other kisses that preceded it.

Their first kiss, and the second one that soon followed along with the endless kisses of that afternoon, were the recognition of strangers as no longer strangers. It was the first attempt at knowing if their bodies confirmed the hypothesis each had formed about the other and about the briefest story in which they would be the stars.

That kiss was the natural and ancient ritual of probing the tastes and intentions of that boy and that girl as they ate their lips and pushed their way into each other with tenderness and eagerness, as wetness began in the parting lips and the river flowed downward until the dampness went lower, and their chests beat and sweat ran down their valleys.

The river found its way, as it always has, to their core. And its force drew them together from mouth to mouth, from body to body, from hand to hand.

That kiss of long ago was the kiss of always, against which all other kisses have and will be measured and compared. It was the sign and it was the tattoo that stayed regardless of where they might be in time and place. It was the seal of each other's approval as the new and better half of each other.

The kiss was also a dance to the slowest movement of their music. As they danced to this wonderful lullaby, their eyes illuminated even as they tried to keep them shut, wanting to imagine the dance that would follow, the life that could follow this perfect moment. This amazing dance of grace made their breath become one and sighs become their code, one of many they would always recognize as theirs and theirs alone. The kiss was as unique as the imprint now left on their lips and in their mouths and on their tongues that spoke to their counterpart, dancing their very own dance.

It was the kiss we all seek and the kiss for which we all walk the Earth. It was the kiss of a thousand Juliets and a thousand Romeos just before death.

It was the first kiss of Rhett and Scarlett before the war changed the soul of the South, a time when they still, frankly, gave a damn.

It was also the cautious kiss of Santomé and Avellaneda during the truce that God granted them and then viciously took away that dark September afternoon in Montevideo.

The kiss was a kiss that once took place between Robert, the photographer, and Francesca, the farmer's wife, one sultry evening by those old bridges in Iowa.

And, too, it was the kiss bought and turned to magic by the charming woman of the night, Vivian, who along with her prince, Edward, came together on that seedy corner in Hollywood and unexpectedly wrote a fairytale.

It was the first kiss in their lives and the last kiss that came from heaven. It was, by their definition, endless. It was a fragile kiss caught between them as acrobats holding onto each other perilously above the ground.

It was the kiss, as legend has it, through which an angel passed by silently.

Like all the billions of trillions of kisses before this one, it was as much a beginning as it was an end for the simple yet endless story of that boy and that girl.

Keith

After reading the poem again, Abby asked herself the same question she had asked herself the first time she read it: *Did I ever love someone like this? Was there ever a kiss like that in my life? Would someone have written something like this about me?*

The answer was always the same, but it was an answer she would keep to herself. It was like her forever box, for herself only. In it were her questions and, more importantly, her answers of a lifetime. She would keep the certainty of those answers tucked neatly in her heart until her very last breath.

Then sleep came, a night of peaceful rest.

As Abby gradually awakened the following morning, she remembered wondering, part dream and part vague recollection, whether her father, Keith Miller, and her mother, Samantha Riley, *that boy* and *that girl*, had finally found each other somewhere in heaven. On the other side. Somewhere beyond the shape of life as we know it.

As that thought dissipated, she opened her eyes, got slowly out of bed, and started her day.

She walked to the windows and opened the blinds to visit her old friend the ocean, sitting still and vast before her. It was this view that had convinced her to leave New York and breathe life into another chapter of her journey. She knew that when her last breath came, she'd like for it to be as she gazed into the blue water from this very room. And, as she had since childhood, she wondered for a moment if someone stood at the other side of the sea, looking at the horizon, wondering who was on the coast on the other side.

About the Author

An ad agency executive by day, David Ravelo has been writing poetry, essays, and articles for years in the shadows. Although not a native Texan, he couldn't get there fast enough to make it home. He plays tennis and music every chance he gets. Not at the same time, but always with gusto. He is the father of a young girl, Carla Louella, always his companion, always his true north. He is often seen around, here and there, with a guitar in one hand and his daughter in the other. Rumor has it he's been seen chasing a beautiful and exotic woman by the name of Mahnaz. *There Love Lies* is his second novel.

www.ingramcontent.com/pod-product-compliance
Lightning Source LLC
Chambersburg PA
CBHW051636260626
47170CB00004B/1194